A
SYRUP OF THE BEES

(भृंगीशसुघाभृत्पुषा)

TRANSLATED FROM THE ORIGINAL MANUSCRIPT

BY

F. W. BAIN

Love was the wine, and Jealousy the lees,
Bitter of brine, and syrup of the bees.

WITH A FRONTISPIECE

METHUEN & CO. LTD.
36 ESSEX STREET, W.C.
LONDON

TO

MRS. THEODORE BECK

PREFACE

THE Young Barbarians, when Rome's ecclesiastical polity got hold of them, were persuaded by their anxious foster-mother to sell their Scandinavian birthright of imagination for an unintelligible, theopathic mess of mystic Græco-Syrian pottage. But the "demons," though driven generally from the field, lurked about in holes and corners, watching their opportunity. They took refuge in bypaths, leaving the high road: they lay in ambush in a thicket, whence nothing ever could dislodge them : that of fairy tales and fables.

In India, the "demons," *i.e.* the fairy tales and fables, have never had to hide. But the fairy tales of India differ from the fairy tales of England, much as their fairies do themselves. The fairies of Europe are children, little people : and it is to children that fairy stories are addressed. The child is the agent, as well as the appeal. In India it is otherwise : the fairy stories are addressed to the grown-up, and the fairies resemble their audience : they are grown up too. They form an intermediate, and so to say, irresponsible class of beings, half-way between the mortals and the gods. These last two are very serious things : they have their work to do : not so the fairies, who exist as it were for the sake of existence—"art for art's sake"—and have nothing to do but what people who have nothing to do always do do—to get themselves and other people into mischief. They are distinguished by three noteworthy characteristics. In the first place, they are *possessors of the sciences*, *i.e.* magic, and this it is which gives them their proper name (*Widyádhara*),[1] which is almost equivalent to our *wizard*. Secondly, every Widyádhara can change his shape at will into anything he pleases : they are all *shape-changers* (*Kámarupa*). And finally, their element is air : they live in the air, and are thus denominated *sky-goers*, *sky-roamers*, *air-wanderers*, in innumerable synonyms. These are the peculiar attributes of the fairies of Ind.

[1] Some kindly critics of these stories have objected to the W, here or elsewhere. The answer to this is, that European scholars have taught everybody to pronounce everything wrong, by *e.g.* introducing into Sanskrit a letter that it does not contain. There is no V in Sanskrit, nor can any Hindoo, without special training, pronounce it : he says, for instance, *walwe* for *valve*.

Like many other persons in India (and out of it) who are far from being either fairies or wizards, they are extraordinarily touchy, and violently resentful of scorn or slight: things not nice to anybody, but the Wizards are not Christians, and generally take dire revenge. A very trifling provocation will set them in a flame. The Widyádharí lady is jealousy incarnate. Jealousy, be it noted, is a thing that many people much misunderstand. Ask anyone the question, where in literature is jealousy best illustrated, and ninety-nine people in a hundred will reply, Othello. But, as Pushkin excellently says, Othello is not naturally a jealous man at all: he is his exact antipodes, a confiding, unsuspicious nature.[1] Jealousy not only distrusts on evidence; it distrusts before evidence and without it; it anticipates evidence and condemns without a trial: it does not wait even for "trifles light as air," but constructs them for itself out of nonentity. Its essence is causeless and irrational suspicion. Your true jealous nature never trusts anything or anybody for an instant. Othello is of noble soul: no jealous man ever was or could be. With women, it is not quite the same; but even here,

[1] This "detached reflection" of Russia's national poet is endorsed by Dostoyeffsky, the greatest master of jealousy that the world has ever seen.

real nobility of character excludes the possibility of
jealousy, because it trusts, until it is deceived, and
then its glass is shattered, and its love gone beyond
recall : sympathy is annihilated. Compare Mary
Queen of Scots and Elizabeth : the one, the noblest,
the other, the meanest creature that ever sat upon a
throne. Mary trusted even Darnley till she discovered
that he was beneath every sentiment but one : Good
Queen Bess never trusted anyone at all. *Mauvaise
espèce de femme !*

And so, they are not much to be depended on, these
Wizards ; anybody taking up with one of them, male
or female, had better be careful. You can never tell
where you are with them ; their affection is unstable ;
they are fickle, as might be expected from creatures
of the air : their feelings are as variable as their shapes.
They can be just as hideously ugly as unimaginably
beautiful. The stories that deal with them contain
a moral entirely in harmony with all Indian ideas :
it is a mistake not to stick to your own caste. When
two of different castes are thrown together, the trouble
inevitably begins. The gipsies, who came apparently
from Sind, brought this notion into Europe, in a
form not previously familiar to it. That difference of
kind is insurmountable, is the fundamental axiom of
Indian theory and practice. The owl to the owl, the

crow to the crow : otherwise, Nemesis and catastrophe. *A Syrup of the Bees*[1] is another instance.

Everywhere to-day we hear people singing a very different song : from all sides is dinned into our ears the cant of humanity, "our common humanity." In the meantime, men differ in many ways more than they agree, and the differences of humanity are practically far more vital than the common base. Just as, though all men have weight, yet gravitation simply by reason of its universality does not constitute an element of politics, and is altogether a negligible quantity, fact though it be, so is it with humanity : the generic identity is nothing, the peculiar distinctions all. The world is not like a plain, but an irregular region such as that of the Alps or Himalaya, consisting of inaccessible peaks that separate deep valleys, at the bottom of which live parcels of humanity drowned in thick fogs or mists of totally different colours and intensities, that distort and transmogrify everything they see : so that if here and there any single individual succeeds in climbing, by dint of toil or special circumstances, to the tops, where in the clear ether all the situation lies

[1] The title has a secondary meaning (with reference to its place in the series), *she that is loaded with the nectar of Maheshwara, i.e.* the moon that he wears.

spread out in its truth before his eye, he will find that he has thereby only cut himself absolutely off from communion and sympathy, not only with the denizens of his own valley, but that of all the others too. From that moment he ceases to be intelligible to the rest. No reasoning of his can ever touch them, or succeed in opening their eyes, because their error is not one of reason, but of perception : they cannot, because they do not, see things as he sees them : the mists,[1] with all their refraction and delusive transformation, are always there. Say what he will, he will not awake them : he will gain nothing in return for all his efforts but ridicule, abuse, or neglect. So Disraeli, in his generation, seemed to himself to be like one pouring, from a golden goblet, water upon sand. To be above the level of humanity is to be counted, till after you are dead, as one who is below.

And this is the exact condition in the India of to-day. The irony of fate has thrown together, as though by some vast geological convulsion, the dwellers in two valleys, one of whom sees everything through, so to say, a red mist, and the other through a blue : they move about and mix in a way together,

---

[1] No mere learning will remove them. Pundits, as a rule, end where they began, "lost in the gloom of uninspired research."

totally unable to see things in the same light : and all
the while this melancholy cuckoo-cry of *common
humanity* fills the air with its reiteration, and people
persist in handling the situation with a wilful and
almost criminal determination to ignore what stares
them in the face, and by so doing, still further
accentuate the very thing they will not see. If you
take two men who are infinitely far from being
brothers, and forcibly unite them, on the pretext that
they are, you will produce by irritation an enmity
between them that would never have existed, had they
been let alone.

I stood, a little while since, on the very edge of a
plateau, that fell down sheer four thousand feet or
more, into the valley of Mysore. Far in the distance
to the north, the dense dark green forest jungle
stretched away like a carpet, intersected here and
there by Moyar's silver streams, with here and there a
velvet boss, where a rounded hill stood up out of the
plain. That carpet, as it seemed from the height, so
uniform and close in its texture, is made of great trees,
under which wander wild elephants in herds. To
right and left, the valley ran both ways out of sight,
like a monster chasm with one side removed. And in
the air below, above, around, light wreaths and ragged

fragments of cloud and mist floated and streamed and drifted, casting the most beautifully deep blue shifting shadows not only on the earth, but on the air, like waterfalls of colour, half hiding and half framing the distant view, and cutting the sunlight into intermittent fountains of a golden semi-purple rain that fell and changed, now here, now there, now, as you looked upon them, gone, now suddenly shooting out elsewhere to transform every colour that they touched into something other than it was, like a magic show suddenly thrown out by the Creator in the silent and unfrequented solitude of his hills, for sheer delight and as it were simply for his own amusement, not caring in the least whether there might be any eye open to catch and worship such a beautiful profusion of his power, or not.   For, strange ! the spell and mysterious appeal of all such momentary glimpses lies, not in what you see, but in what you do not hear : it is the dead silence, the stillness, that by a paradox seems to be the undertone, or background, of moving mist and lonely mountain peaks.

So as I stood, gazing, there came suddenly from the east, a whisper, a mutter ; a low sound, that suggested a distant mixture of wind and sea.   And I turned round, and looked, and I saw a sight that I never shall see again ; such a sight as a man can hardly

expect to see twice, in the time of a single life. Rain
—but was it rain?—rain in a terrific wall, a dark
precipice of appalling gloom, rain that rose like a
colossal curtain from earth to heaven and north to
south, was coming up the valley straight towards me,
and it struck me, as I saw it, with a thrill that was
almost dread. That was what the people saw, long
ago, when the Deluge suddenly came upon them. It
came on, steadily, swiftly, like a thing with orders to
carry out, and a purpose to fulfil, cutting the valley
athwart with the edge of its solid front, sharp as that
of a knife laid on a slice of bread : a black ominous
mass of elemental obliteration, out of which there
came a voice like the rushing of a flood and the beating
of wings, mixed with a kind of wail, like the noise of
the cordage of a ship, in a gale at sea. It blotted out
creation, and in the phrase of old Herodotus, day
suddenly became night. A moment later, I stood in
whirling rain and fog that made sight useless a yard
away, as wet as one just risen from the sea, with a soul
on the very verge of cursing the Creator, for so abruptly
dropping the curtain on his show : forgetting, in my
ingratitude, first, the favour he had done me ; secondly,
how many were those who had not seen ; lastly, and
above all, that it was the very dropping of that
stupendous curtain that gave its finishing touch and

climax to the show. For he knows best, after all. Introduce into Nature were it but a single atom of stint, of parsimony, of preservation, of regret for loss ; and the power, and with it, the sublimity of the infinite is gone. Were Nature to pose, to attitudinise for contemplation, even for the fraction of a second, she would annihilate the condition on which reposes all her charm. Ruthless destruction, even of her own choicest works, is the badge of her inexhaustible omnipotence : add but a touch of pity, and you fall back to the littleness and feebleness of man.

And I mused, as I departed : how can that be communicated to others, which cannot even be described at all ? And if so, in the things of the body, how much more with the things of the soul ? Who shall convey to the souls that stumble and jostle in the foggy valleys, any glimpse of the visions, denied to them, above ; any spark of comprehension of the things that they might discern, on the tops of the pure and silent hills, that stand uncomprehended, kissing heaven above the fog ?

POONA, 1914

CONTENTS

I

A TWILIGHT EPIPHANY

A

I

A TWILIGHT EPIPHANY

The three worlds worship the sound of the string that twanged of old like the hum of bees [1] as it slipped from faint Love's faltering hand and fell at his feet unstrung, the bow unbent and the shaft unsped, as if to beg for mercy from that other shaft of scorching flame that shot from the bow-despising brow of the moony-crested god.

FAR down in the southern quarter, at the very end of the Great Forest, just where the roots of its outmost trees are washed by the waves of the eastern sea, there was of old a city, which stood on the edge of land and water, like as the evening moon hangs

[1] The bowstring of Love's bow is made of a line of bees. Love was reduced to ashes by fire from Shiwa's extra eye, for audaciously attempting to subject that great ascetic to his own power.

where light and darkness meet. And just outside
the city wall where the salt sand drifts in the wind,
there was a little old ruined empty temple of the
Lord of the Moony Tire, whose open door was as
it were guarded by two sin-destroying images of the
Deity and his wife, one on the right of the threshold
and the other on the left, looking as if they had
suddenly started asunder, surprised by the crowd of
devotees, to make a way between. And on an
evening long ago, when the sun had finished
setting, Maheshwara was returning from Lanká to
his own home on Kailás, with Umá in his arms. So
as he went, he looked down, and saw the temple
away below. And he said to his beloved: Come,
now, let us go down, and revisit this little temple,
which has stood so long without us. And it looks
white in the moon's rays, as if it had turned pale, for
fear that we have forgotten it.

So when they had descended, Maheshwara said
again: See how these two rude and mutilated effigies
that are meant for thee and me stand, as it were,
waiting, like bodies for their souls. Let us enter in,
and occupy, and sanctify these images,[1] and rest for a
little while, before proceeding to thy father's peaks.

---

[1] The real divinity of a Hindoo temple is not the images
outside on its walls, but the symbol (whatever it be) inside.

And if I am not mistaken, our presence will be opportune, and this deserted temple will presently be visited by somebody who stands in sore need of our assistance, which as long as they remain untenanted these our images cannot give him, since they have even lost their hands.[1] And accordingly they entered, each into his own image, and remained absolutely still, as though the stone was just the stone it always was, and nothing more. And yet those stony deities glistened in the full moon's light, as though the presence of deity had lent them lustre of their own, that laughed as though to say : See, now we are as white as the very foam at our feet.

So as they stood, silent, and listening to the sound of the sea, all at once there came a man who ran towards them. And taking off his turban, he cast it at the great god's feet, and fell on his face himself. And after a while, he looked up, and joined his hands, and said : O thou Enemy of Love, now there is absolutely no help for me but in the sole of thy foot. For when the sun rose this morning, the Queen was found lying drowned, and all broken to pieces, in the sea foam under the palace wall. And when they

---

[1] A common feature throughout India. Everywhere they went, the devotees of the Koràn used to smash and maim the Hindoo idols.

ran to tell the King, they found him also lying dead, where he sleeps on his palace roof that hangs over the sea, with a dagger in his heart. And the city is all in uproar, for loss to understand it, and Gangádhara the minister has made of me a victim, by reason of an old grudge. And now my head will be the forfeit, unless I can discover the guilty before the rising of another sun. And thou who knowest all things, past, present, or to come, art become my only refuge. Grant me, of thy favour, a boon, and reveal to me the secret, for who but thyself can possibly discover how the King and Queen have come to this extraordinary end.

So as he spoke, gazing as if in desperation at Maheshwara, all at once, as if moved to compassion, that image of the Deity turned from the wall towards him, and nodded at him its stony head: so that in his terror that unhappy mortal nearly left his own body, and fell to the ground in a swoon. And Maheshwara gazed at him intently, as he lay, and put him, by his *yoga*,[1] asleep. And the Daughter of the Snow said softly: O Moony-crested, who is this unlucky person, and what is the truth of this whole matter, for I am curious to know? And Maheshwara

---

[1] What we should call, in such a case, mesmerism : the power of concentrated will. There is something in it, after all.

said slowly: O Snowy One, this is the chief of the night watch of the city; and be under no alarm. For while he sleeps, I will reveal the truth to him, in a magic dream: making him as it were a third person, to overhear our conversation. And I will do the same to the prime minister, so that in the morning, finding their two dreams tally, he will gain credit and save his life. Thereupon Párwatí said again: O Lord of creation, save mine also. For I am as it were dying of curiosity, to hear how all this came about.

So then, after a while, that omniscient Deity said slowly: All this has come about, by reason of a dream. And Gauri said: How could a dream be the cause of death, both to the King and Queen? Then said Maheshwara: Not only is there danger in dreaming, but the greatest. Hast thou not seen thy father's woody sides reflected in the still mirror of his own tarns? And the goddess said: What then? And Maheshwara said: Hast thou not marked how the reflection painted on the water contains beauty, drawn as it were from its depths, greater by far than does the very thing it echoes, of which it is nothing but an exact copy? And Párwatí said: Aye, so it does. Then said Maheshwara: So it is with dreams. For their danger lies in this very beauty, and like pictures upon quiet water, which contains absolutely nothing at all, below, they show men, sleeping, visions of unrealisable beauty, which, being nothing whatever but copies of what they have seen, awake, possess notwithstanding an additional fascination, not to be found in the originals, which fills them with insatiable longing and an utter contempt of all that their waking life contains, as in the present instance : so that they sacrifice all in pursuit of a hollow phantom, trying to achieve impossibility, by bringing mind-begotten dream into the sphere of reality, whither it cannot enter but by ceasing to be dream. But the worst of all is, as in this King's case, when dreaming is intermingled with the reminiscences of a former birth : for then it becomes fatality. And Párwatí said : How is that ? Then said Maheshwara : Every soul that is born anew lies buried in oblivion, having utterly forgotten all its previous existence, which has become for it as a thing that has never been. And yet, sometimes, when impressions are very vivid, and memory very strong, here and there an individual soul, steeped as it were in the vat of its own experience, and becoming permanently dyed, as if with indigo, will laugh, so to say, at oblivion, and carry over indelible impressions, from one birth to another, and so live on, haunted by dim recollections that throng his memory like ghosts, and resembling one striving vainly to recall the loveliness and colour of a flower of which he can remember absolutely nothing but the scent, whose lost fragrance hangs about him, goading memory to ineffectual effort, and thus filling him with melancholy which he can never either dispel or understand.

So as he spoke, there came past the temple door a young man of the Shabara caste, resembling a tree for his height, carrying towards the forest a young woman of slender limbs, who was struggling as he held her, and begging to be released; to which he answered only by laughing as he held her tighter, and giving her every now and then a kiss as he went along, so that as they passed by, there fell from her hair a *champak* flower, which lay on the ground unheeded after they disappeared. And the Daughter of the Mountain exclaimed: See, O Moony-crested, this flower laid as it were at thy feet as a suppliant for her protection: for this is a case for thy interference, to save innocence from evil-doing.

And Maheshwara looked at her with affection in his smile. And he said : Not so, O mountain-born : thou art deceived : since this is a case where inter-ference would be bitterly resented, not only by the robber, but his prey : for notwithstanding all her feigned reluctance, this slender one is inwardly delighted, and desires nothing less than to be taken at her word. For this also is a pair of lovers, who resemble very closely those other lovers, whose story I am just about to tell thee : as indeed all lovers are very much the same. For Love is tyranny, and the essence of the sweetness of its nectar is a despotic authority that is equally delicious to master and to slave. For just as every male lover loves to play the tyrant, so does every woman love to play the slave, so much, that unless her love contains for her the consciousness of slavery, it is less than nothing in her own eyes, and she does not love at all. And know, that as nothing in the world is so hateful to a woman as force, exerted on her by a man she does not love, so nothing fills her with such supreme intoxication as to be masterfully made by her lover to go along the road of her own inclination, since so she gets her way without seeming to consent, and is extricated from the dilemma of deciding between her scruples and her wish. For indecision is the very nature of every woman, and it is a torture to her, to decide, no matter how. And even when she does decide, she does so, generally as a victim, driven by circumstances or desperation, and never as a judge, as in the case of both those women who determined the destiny of this dead King, the one deciding in his favour, precisely because he would allow her no choice, and the other very much against him indeed: and yet both, so to say, without any good reason at all. For women resemble yonder waves of the sea, things compounded of passion and emotion, with impulses for arguments, and agitation for energy, for ever playing, fretting and moaning with laughter and tears of brine and foam : and like feminine incarnations of the instability of water, one and the same essence running through a multitude of contradictory and beautiful qualities and forms : being cold and hard as ice, and soft and white as snow, and still as pools, and crooked as rivers, now floating in heaven like clouds and mists and vapours, and now plunging, like cataracts and waterfalls, into the abyss of hell. Is not the same water bitter as death to the drowning man, and sweeter than a draught of nectar, saving the life of the traveller dying of thirst in the desert sand.

So, now, listen, while I tell thee the story of this King.

And as he began to speak, the wind fell, and the sea slumbered, and the moon crept silently further up and up the sky. And little by little, the dark shadows stole out stealthily, moving as it were on tiptoe, and hung in corners, here and there, like ghosts about the little shrine, before which the sleeping man lay white in the moon's rays, as still as if he were a corpse. And the deep tones of the Great God's voice seemed like a muttered spell, to lull to sleep the living and assemble the dead to hear, with demons for *dwárapálas* at the door of an ashy tomb.

II

AN INCOMPLETE OBLIVION

II

AN INCOMPLETE OBLIVION

I

KNOW, then, that this King, who was found dead in the early morning, with a dagger in his heart, was named Arunodaya.[1] For his father said, when he was born: This son is, as it were, the sunrise of our hopes. And yet, by the decree of destiny, it turned out altogether contrary to his expectation. For as it happened, his father, in whose family it was an hereditary custom to have only one queen at a time, grew gradually tired of his only wife. But being as cowardly in crime as he was weak in constancy, he did not dare to bring about his wishes by any violence or practice of his own, but lay as it were in wait, for some suitable opportunity or occasion to present

[1] (Pronounce *daya* as *die*, with accent on preceding *o*.) It means *the rising of red dawn*.

itself, by means of which he might succeed in getting rid of her, without incurring any blame, or running any risk. For such souls as his was, think to throw dust in the eyes of Chitragupta,[1] not knowing that he does but add cowardice to the total of their guilt.

So while he waited, time went on, and year succeeded year. And little by little he and his queen grew gradually older, and his son changed slowly from a boy into a man.

And then, at last, one day it happened, that the King and Queen were sitting together on the palace roof. And all at once, the Queen started to her feet with a cry. And as the King looked towards her, with wonder and curiosity, she said slowly: Aryaputra,[2] know, that I have suddenly recollected my former birth. And now, I long to tell thee all about it; and yet I am afraid. For this is the law, that if anybody suddenly remembers his former birth, and tells it to another, that very moment he must die. And if I die, I must leave thee: for if not, what could death do to me, since that is the only thing in the three worlds of which I am afraid?

---

[1] The Recorder, who keeps account of all the sins that each soul must answer for, at the end of every birth.

[2] i.e. *son of a nobleman*, the term used by a queen in addressing her husband.

So as she looked at him, with regret and affection in her eyes—for she was as devoted to her husband as if he had been worthy, as indeed he was utterly unworthy, of her devotion—all at once the King's heart leaped in his breast. And he said to himself: Ha! Here, as it seems, is that very opportunity, for which I have been waiting all these years: till I thought that my soul would almost part from my body, for sheer impatience and disgust. And in an instant, he also sprang to his feet, exclaiming as he did so, with an ecstasy that was only half feigned: Strange! can it be? For I, too, have suddenly remembered my former birth: as if this recollection of thine had been the spark required, to set fire to the memory of my own. So now, then, let us very quickly tell each other all, and so take leave together of these miserable bodies, into which we must, beyond a doubt, have fallen, by reason of a curse.

So then, deceived by the display of his hypocritical affection, the Queen told him very quickly all that she recollected of her former birth. And when she had finished, the King looked at her steadily for a while, and his face fell. And he said, with difficulty: Alas! alas! I was utterly mistaken: and as I think, I took fire falsely, out of sympathy with thee. And now I have fallen unwittingly into an irreparable disaster. For

B

as to my own former birth, I remember absolutely nothing about anything at all.

So as he spoke, he looked at the Queen, and their eyes met. And in that instant, she understood ; and caught, like a flash of lightning, the falsehood in his soul. And she gazed at him, for a while, fixedly, with eyes that resembled an incarnation of scrutiny that was mingled with reproach, till all at once he turned away, unable to endure the detection of his own baseness, reflected as it were in the calm mirror of her own pure gaze. And after a while, she said slowly : Son, not of a noble, but an outcast, know, that thou hast doomed not me only, but thyself. And now, because thou hast betrayed me to my death, thy son also shall die as I do, and on the very same spot, by the agency of one who stands to him in the very same relation that I do to thee : and the husband shall pay for the wife. And the consequence of works shall dog thee, in the form of the total extinction of thy race. But as for me, now I see only too clearly that this birth has been a blunder, and a punishment, and a delusion, resembling a scene played upon a stage, whose king turns out, when the curtain falls, to be but a sorry rascal after all. And all the while, I have given my devotion to the wrong husband, and like a foolish benefactor, have wasted alms on a pitiful impostor. I feared, but one short moment since, to leave thee, and to part from thee; but now, thou hast suddenly changed regret into relief. See, whether separation will be thy blessing or thy curse.

So as she spoke, she tottered, and her soul suddenly left its body, which sank to the ground abandoned, like a creeper that collapses when the trunk it clung to falls, and saying as if to mock him: Seek now for the core that is gone, within the hollow husk.

II

So then, when her funeral obsequies were over, that widowed King, strange to say! fell into melancholy, deceiving all his subjects, as if by express design. For they pitied him exceedingly, each saying to the other: See, now, how this good Queen's death has robbed this poor deserted King as it were of his own soul: as well, indeed, it might. For she was a *patidewata*,[1] and a Sawitri, not only in her name, but in her nature, and rather than outlive him, preferred to go before. Whereas, on the contrary, that King's decline arose, not from regret, but from

[1] i.e. *a wife who makes a god of her husband:* the highest of all possible praises. Sawitri is the Hindoo Alcestis.

remorse, mixed with anxiety and the apprehension of his coming doom. For this is the way of the weak, that they yield to evil impulse, and yet repent of their own doings, taking fright at the sight of them, as soon as they are done, and discovering the terrible consequences of works, too late. For a deed that is done, is divided from what it was, before it was done, by all eternity, in the fraction of a second : as this King found to his cost. For even as he gazed at the body of his queen, lying dead on the floor beside him, remorse rose up as it were out of her body and took him by the throat. And at that moment, he would have thrown away his kingdom like a blade of grass, to bring her back to life. And his longing to get rid of her changed, like a flash of lightning, into a passionate yearning to repossess her, dead. And he said to himself, as he looked at her : Where in the world shall I find another resembling her in the least degree, and what shall I do, to save myself from the ripening of her curse ? For destiny listens in silence to the prayers of a pure woman, and she, beyond all doubt, was one.

So then, from that very moment, every thought of replacing her by another queen abandoned him, as if her life, in leaving her, had drawn with it his own. And all his taste for life at all, and all desires whatever, suddenly left him in a body, as if out of disgust at his behaviour. And he sank into despair, and pined and waned like an old moon, and grew gradually dimmer, and thinner, and more gloomy, till there was hardly anything left of him at all, but skin and bone. And finally, seeing its opportunity, a burning fever arising from a chill entered in and took possession of all his limbs, as if to give him a foretaste of the flames of his own pyre.

And then at last, perceiving that Yama had caught him in his noose, and finding himself in the mouth of death, he summoned his prime minister, together with his son. And when they came, he said to them: Since I am on the very point of following my wife, as, had I gone before her, she would have followed me, *sati*[1] that she was, there is no time to lose. Do thou, my son, get married, as quickly as thou canst, for the god of death has clutched us both, as if he was in a hurry, just at the very moment when we were thinking of procuring thee a wife. And as it is, I am sore afraid of going to meet my

---

[1] *Sati*, which means *a good woman*, is always understood by Europeans to refer to what is only the last manifestation of her quality, the burning herself on her dead lord's pyre. But the term does not necessarily contain any reference to that stern climax of her virtue.

ancestors, who will angrily reproach me for placing them in jeopardy, by neglecting to provide for them in time. And when they ask me, saying: Where is thy son's son? what answer shall I make? And therefore, O my minister, I leave this son of mine and his marriage as a deposit in thy hands, which I shall require of thee in the other world. Postpone all other policy to the duty of finding him a wife: and if thou canst, let her resemble his mother, that was mine.

So having spoken, in a little while he died, leaving everybody in his kingdom wondering at his affection for his wife. For nobody knew the truth, which was as it were burned up and utterly annihilated by the fires that consumed the body of his wife and his own. And he left behind him a reputation for fidelity that was absolutely false. For none but the Deity can penetrate the disguise of hypocrisy. And yet, though he deceived all the subjects in his kingdom, he did not succeed in blinding the eyes of Dharma,[1] who caught his soul in his noose, and doomed it, for his treachery, to be born again in the body of a worm.

[1] Another name for Yama, the god of death, which we may here take as equivalent to "Justice."

III

So, then, when his funeral obsequies were over, and the due time prescribed by the *shastras* had elapsed, his son Arunodaya mounted the throne, and became king in his room. And no sooner was the crown placed upon his head, and the water sprinkled over him, than the prime minister, who was named Gangádhara, came to him privately, and said: Maháráj, now there is yet another ceremony which remains as it were crying to be performed, with the least possible delay; and that is thy own marriage. And now it is for thee and me to seek out some maiden that will make a royal match for thee, and lead her round the fire, and so let thy father's spirit rest. And there cannot be any difficulty at all. For all the neighbouring kings, who possess daughters, are watching thee like clouds around a mountain top, ready to rain daughters as it were upon thy head; since thou art superior in power to them all. And as for the daughters, the painters, and the rumours of thy beauty, have turned them all into so many *abhisárikas*, dying to run into thy arms without waiting to be asked; and the only danger is, that all but the one on whom thy choice shall fall will immediately abandon the body, out of jealousy and despair, as soon as it is made. For everybody knows that even Ananga and Rati [1] were envious of thy father and thy mother; of whom thou art compounded into an essence twice as powerful as either was alone, so that not a day passes but my spies bring me news of miserable women who have deserted the body of their own accord, finding themselves, by reason of their caste or condition, cut off from all hope of ever becoming thy wife.

Then said Arunodaya: O Gangádhara, I am ready to marry in a moment any one of them : and yet, as I think, I shall never marry anyone at all. And Gangádhara said: Maháráj, thou speakest riddles, and I am slow to understand. And Arunodaya looked at him with a smile. And he said: Gangádhara, it is proper that a minister should know all his master's secrets, and now that thou art my minister, I will tell thee mine, and make thee my confidant in everything, as expediency demands. For then only will the business of our policy run on smoothly, when we pull exactly together, like a pair of bullocks in a cart. And whether it be with the women as thou sayest, or not, there is a difficulty, unknown to thee, on my part. Then said the

---

[1] *i.e.* the God of Love and his principal wife.

minister: What is that? And Arunodaya said: I am already more than half married, and, as it were, bound, by an indissoluble pledge, to an undiscoverable beauty; and unless she can be found, I am, as I told thee, likely to remain unmarried for the remainder of my life.

Then said the prime minister: Maháráj, everything can be found by one who looks for it in the proper place. And if thy beauty be discoverable, I will undertake to find her, at the forfeit of my head. And who, then, is she? Give me at least a clue; and thou shalt see, that maybe she is not hidden so very far away, after all.

And Arunodaya said: I will marry no other woman but the wife of my former birth. For I dream of her, and as it seems to me, have dreamed of her, and nothing else, ever since I was born. And so, now, I have revealed to thee a secret, which I never told to anyone but thee: and I leave thee to judge, whether she is able to be found, or not. And if thou canst show me that any one of these kings' daughters was my wife before, I will marry her again: but this is the indispensable condition; and no matter who she may be, the woman who does not fulfil it must marry some one other than myself. And now, go: and when thou hast meditated sufficiently on the matter, return to me at dawn, and take counsel with me, as to what is to be done. For, as thou seest, this marriage of mine is not likely to be easily achieved. And I resemble one searching on the sea-shore for a grain of sand, dropped there in the dead of night, a hundred years ago.

IV

So then, that astounded prime minister gazed at Arunodaya for a while in silence, and took his dismissal, and went away like a man in a dream. And when he reached his home, he sat for a long time musing, like a picture painted on a wall. And then, all at once, he began to laugh. And he exclaimed: Ha! this, then, was the secret, and now at length I begin to understand, and all is explained. For this young king *brahmachári,*[1] little as he suspects it, has been under my eye ever since he was born. And this, then, was the reason why he was perpetually wandering about alone, and lying for hours gazing at the lotuses in the forest pools, or looking at the sea-waves, like a rock on the shore, differing totally

[1] As we might say, *bachelor,* but the Hindoo expression is stricter, meaning, *one who has taken a vow of virginity.*

from all others of his kind, who as a rule resemble *must* elephants, in utterly refusing to have anything to do with dancing girls or women of any kind, as it were wilfully contradicting the design of the Creator, who beyond a doubt formed him on purpose to prevent Rati and Priti [1] from quarrelling, by providing a second body for their common lord. And all the while I took him for a very *yogi*, he was, as it turns out, dreaming, not of emancipation, but this wife of his former birth : and hard as it is, I think that even emancipation would, of the two, be easier to attain. Well might he say, that she was difficult to find. For who ever got at the wife of his former birth, except in a dream. Aye! this is an obstacle to his marriage indeed, that even the Lord of the Elephant-Face would be puzzled to surmount or remove.

And after a while, he said again : Is it a mere fancy? Or can it be, that he really is haunted by some dim recollection of his former wife, since beyond a doubt the influences of pre-existence do sometimes persist, and like ships, sail without sinking over the dark ocean of oblivion, from one birth-island to another? And what, then, is she like? For could I only discover what she looks like in his dreams, it might be that by policy or stratagem I could make

[1] The two wives of Love.

shift to find her, or somebody so like her that he would never know the difference. I will go to him to-morrow and ask him to describe her, and he cannot well refuse. For how can he expect me to discover her, unless I know what she is like? Or can it be, that he does not even know himself? That would be better still. For then, if, with the assistance of the astrologers, I can manage to devise a scheme, so as to persuade him that I have lit upon that which he is looking for, how could he detect the imposition? There are only too many kings' daughters who would think that the very fruit of their birth was gained, by practising so innocent a deception as to pass for the wife of his former birth in order to become in very truth his wife in this. And if I cannot succeed in some dexterous trick of substitution, I shall be almost ready to abandon the body myself, for sheer exasperation. For even apart from the necessity of getting him married, there is not one of the surrounding kings who is not ready to throw a crore of gold pieces at my head, if only I will even promise to become his partisan against all the rest, and marry Arunodaya to some daughter of his own. Out upon it, that with kings' daughters lying thick as lotuses all round him, and ready and even eager to be plucked, this unhappy longing of the king for an unattainable *párijáta* flower should make them all of no more value than withered leaves! O Rider on the Mouse,[1] come to my assistance, for without thy help we shall all be swallowed by calamity, in the form of the utter extinction of this perverse king's kingdom and his race.

V

Now, just at this very moment, it happened, by the decree of destiny, that one of the kings of the Widyádharas,[2] who was rightly named Mahídhara, for his home was on a mountain top that stood in a far-off island beyond the rising sun, was holding a *swayamwara* for all his hundred daughters. And for ninety-nine days each daughter chose her husband, one a day, from out of the suitors who flocked to the marriage in such numbers that the sky looked like a cart-wheel, with lines of Widyádharas assembling from all directions, like vultures, for its spokes. And finally the hundredth day, and with it, the turn of the youngest daughter came, to choose.

Now this daughter resembled a thorn, fixed by the Creator in the hearts of all her sisters, causing perpetual irritation, like a rebel chief in a united

[1] *i.e.* Ganesha.　　　　[2] See Preface.

kingdom. For she stood aloof from them all, like
a little finger that somehow or other refuses to bend
into the closed hand, being not only the youngest,
but the smallest, and the most perverse, and the
loveliest of all, putting not only all her sisters but every
other Widyádhari to the necessity of acknowledging,
sore against their will, that the presence of her beauty
robbed them of their own, reducing them to confusion, like so many impostors confronted by the
true heir. And her nature was so totally dissimilar
to that of everybody else, that she resembled a thing
made by the Creator standing as it were upon his
head, out of the essence of contradiction : since none
of her own family could ever tell what she would or
would not say, or do, or even where she was. And
even her beauty was as wayward as she was herself.
For one of her eyebrows was always as it were on the
tiptoe of surprise, arrogantly arching a little higher than
the other ; and her eyes were very long, with corners
that looked as if they were on the very point of turning
upwards, which none the less they never did, as if
expressly to disappoint and deride the expectation
they aroused, and keep it hovering for ever in an
agony of suspense. And her lips always seemed to
smile even when they were not smiling, and her head
was almost always poised a very little on one side,

looking as if it were listening for the far-off mutter of the mischief that lay as it were slumbering in the thunder-cloud hanging low in the heaven of her huge dark eyes, whose lashes resembled the long grass that fringes the edge of a forest pool. And her limbs were so slender, and her colour was so pale, in the shadow of the masses of her sable hair, that had it not been for the indigo of her lotus eyes and the vermilion of her lips, she would have resembled a marble incarnation of the beauty of death, or a wraith of mist touched as it hovers in a dark valley by the ashy beam of a waning moon. And, strange! her spell seemed made of moods that always changed, yet never varied, compounded half of shy timidity, and half of proud disdain, like an atmosphere of paradoxical fascination, formed of the rival fragrances of sandal-wood and camphor, translated into the language of the soul.

So then, as those Widyádhara suitors waited in the hall, standing round in a ring, she came in slowly, with the garland of choosing in her hand. And beginning with the first she came to, she walked very deliberately all round that circle of excited wooers, going from one to the next in order, and examining each in turn. And in the dead silence, there was absolutely nothing heard but the faint clash of her golden anklets, as she moved round slowly on little hesitating feet, that trod as it were on everybody's heart. And as she went, those suitors, as she came to them and passed them, turned gradually from dark to pale, and then again to black, like the buttresses on the king's high road, when torches pass along.[1] And every Widyádhara's soul abandoned, so to say, his body, on finding that she left him to go on to the next, dooming him as it were to death by carrying further the fatal wreath.

So, then, having given to all, as if by way of boon, a bitter glimpse of beauty mixed with a momentary ray of hope, dashing the cup from each one's lip just as it thought it was going to taste, she came to the very end. And then, she stopped dead. And she looked at them all, for a single moment, over the wreath they all desired, and she raised it to her lips, as if to scent its fragrance, saying as it were to all : Very sweet indeed is the thing beyond your reach. And then, with a little pout, she put it round her own neck. And she said, in the Arya metre :

> Tell me, O breeze, is there syrup for the bees?
> Only, alas ! when kind flowers please.

And then, she went away, leaving all her lovers as it were in the lurch, like a flock of *Chakrawákas* when the sun has disappeared.

[1] This is from Kalidas.

VI

And they all stood, when she had gone, gazing at one another in silence, as motionless as though they had been painted on the walls that stood behind them. And then they all exclaimed, as if with a single voice : What! is not one of us all fit for this fastidious beauty's taste? And instantly that ring of disappointed suitors broke up as they flew away, and vanished like a mist, for in their fury they would not even so much as wait to take leave of her father, counting it as it were a crime in him to be father of such a daughter, and to have lured them into shame. And seeing them go, Mahídhara went himself to the apartments of his daughter. And he said to her in dudgeon: Out on thee! Makarandiká;[1] for here have all the Widyádharas become my bitter enemies by reason of this insult. Has thy reason left thee? Or where wilt thou find a husband, if not even one of all the kings of the Widyádharas can please thy foolish fancy? Dost thou not understand, that a daughter who is not married disgraces her father's house?

Then said Makarandiká: Dear father, I am far too ugly to be married. And Mahídhara laughed, and

---

[1] i.e. *one made of the honey or syrup of flowers.* (Note, that the first syllable rhymes with *luck*, and the third with *fund.*)

he said: What new caprice is this? Thou ugly!
Why, if thou art too ugly, being far the most beautiful
of all, what óf thy sisters, whose beauty all united is
not equal to thy own, and yet have they all chosen?
And Makarandiká laughed, and she exclaimed: What!
can it be? What! shall the most beautiful of all be
content with others' leavings, and choose only out
of what they have all rejected? As if the whole
world were not full to the very brim of husbands!
Shall my choice be the refuse? Moreover, I do not
want a Widyádhara for a husband at all. And
Mahídhara said, with amazement: And why not a
Widyádhara? Then said Makarandiká : Widyádharas
are fickle, and roaming about in the air, come across
all sorts of other women and make love to them,
deceiving their own wives. But I will marry only
such a husband as never will deceive me.

Then said her father, smiling: But, O thou very
jealous maiden, where wilt thou discover him? For
did not even Indra himself play Sachi false? Or
dost thou think that mortal men are always constant,
when even gods are not? Choose, if thou wilt, a
mortal for thy husband, only to discover that Widyádharas are not more treacherous than they are. Thy
husband will deceive thee, as it may be, no matter
what his birth.

And lo! as he looked at her, jesting, he saw her suddenly turn paler, and still paler, as if the very thought resembled poison in her ears. And she said in a low voice: Better never to be married at all, than marry a deceiver: better far for me, and better far for him. And her father exclaimed, in astonishment: What! O Makarandiká! thou hast not even got a husband as yet at all; yet here thou art already, jealous without a cause! What will it be, when thou art actually married? Truly I fear for thy unhappy husband, whoever he may be. And yet, be very careful. Bethink thee, O daughter, that if thou dost choose a mortal, it will be at the cost of thy condition. For any Widyádharí becoming the wife of a mortal man loses all her magic sciences, and is levelled with himself.

And Makarandiká said with scorn: Thy warning is unnecessary, and there is not any risk. For it will be long before I place myself in danger of any such description from a husband of any kind.

VII

So that haughty beauty spoke, ignorant of the future, not dreaming that her destiny in the form of a mortal husband was just about to laugh her vaunt to scorn. And leaving her father abruptly, she rose up into the air, and began to fly swiftly like a wild white swan away towards the western quarter, looking down upon the sea, that resembled a blue mirror of the sky that stretched above it, with foaming waves in place of clouds, and water instead of air: saying to herself: Only let me get away, where not a Widyádhara of them all is to be seen. And the wind caressed her limbs like a lover, stealing embraces as she went along, and whispering in the shell of her little ear: Be not alarmed, O vagrant beauty, if I reveal thy outline to the whole world, for there is nobody by to see. And she watched the sun go down before her, and went on all night long, with no companion but the new moon that sank into the sea in a little while, as if ashamed to rival her, leaving her alone with night. And at last, when dawn was just breaking, she saw below her this very temple, standing alone on the sandy shore between the forest and the sea. And a little further on, the King's palace was standing up like a tower, reddened by the young sun's rays. So, feeling tired, she swooped down, to rest for a little while. And she settled on the edge of the palace roof, taking the form of a snowy bird, with a ruddy bill and legs, as if to mock and imitate the colour of the sun.

And at that very moment, Arunodaya came out upon the roof, with his prime minister behind him, like Winter following the god of Spring. And the very instant she set eyes on him, she became as it were a target for Love's arrow, as if, although invisible, he were there beside his friend.[1] And she fell suddenly in love with the young king as he came towards her, and shook with such agitation, that she came within a very little of falling straight into the sea. And she murmured to herself, with emotion : Can this be a second dawn [2] appearing just to confound the other? Or can it be Kámadewa, in a body more beautiful than his own ? But if so, where is Rati? Or am I only dreaming, having fallen unawares asleep, thinking of husbands and my father's words?

So as she spoke, Arunodaya looked towards her, and presently he said aloud : See, Gangádhara, how yonder snowy sea-bird has come to me as it were for refuge, tired beyond a doubt by some long journey across the sea ! Let us not go too near it, lest out of fright it may take to flight, before its wings are rested. And he sat down a little way off, on the very edge of the terrace, keeping his eye

---

[1] *i.e.* Spring, who is Love's companion.

[2] This is an allusion to the King's name (see note, *ante*) the point of which will presently appear.

on Makarandiká, who laughed at his words in her sleeve, saying softly to herself: There is no fear, O handsome stranger, that I shall fly away, since thy arrival, so far from scaring me away, has nailed me to the spot. And the prime minister said meanwhile: Maháráj, here I am, according to thy appointment, to discuss thy marriage with thee, where nobody can overhear. And know, that since thou art absolutely bent on marrying no other than the wife of thy former birth, I do not despair of finding her, if she is able to be found. But who can find anything, unless he knows what it is like? For if not, he will not know that he has found it, when it lies before his eyes. So tell me, to begin with, what this wife of thine resembles; and then I will set to work and find her, without the loss of any time.

Then Arunodaya said slowly: O Gangádhara, how can I tell thee what I do not know myself? And Gangádhara said, in wonder: Maháráj, it cannot be. How will thou recognise her, not knowing what she looks like? And Arunodaya said again: I shall know her in an instant, the moment I set eyes on her. For at the very sight of her, love, that depends on the forgotten associations of a previous existence, will suddenly shoot up in the darkness of my heart, like flame. For this is the only proof, and no other is required. And yet, there is something else, to give me as it were a clue. For though, strive as I may, I cannot even guess what she was like, yet my memory, as it seems, is not absolutely blank. For I remember, that she was the daughter of a pandit, and maybe herself a pandit; and I seem to listen in a dream, whenever I think about her, to the noise of innumerable pandits, all shouting at the same time some name that I can never catch, mingling with the roar of the waves of the sea.

And when he ended, Gangádhara stared at him, in utter stupefaction, saying within himself: Beyond a doubt, this King is mad. And presently he said aloud: O King Arunodaya, who ever heard of a woman, suited for a king's wife, who had anything to do with pandits? What is there in common between pandits and the wives of kings? Certainly, thou art doomed to live and die unmarried: for a beauty who is a pandit is not to be found in the three worlds.

VIII

Then said Arunodaya: Gangádhara, who knows? But be that as it may, this is absolutely certain, that I will not marry any woman who was not the wife of

my former birth. And so, if thou canst find her, well.
And if not, then thy prophecy will be true, for I shall
live and die without a wife.

And Gangádhara went away again, more at a loss
than he was before. And when he reached his home,
all at once he began to laugh, as if his reason had left
him. And he said to himself: Ha ha! Out on this
unhappy King, who hears the noise of pandits in the
roaring of the sea! Why, even Maheshwara himself
could not find a shout of laughter, to match the
absurdity of this extraordinary jest. And he went on
laughing all day long, till his family grew frightened
and summoned the physicians, saying: He is
possessed.

And meanwhile Makarandiká remained upon the
terrace, watching Arunodaya, as if fascinated by a
snake. And as she listened to their conversation,
her heart beat with such exultation that it shook her
like wind. And she said to herself: Surely I am
favoured by the deity. Well was it for me, that I
scorned to choose a husband from among those
miserable Widyádhara kings: for had I done so, I
should have missed the very fruit of my birth. And
now, by the favour of Ganapati, I have come here in
the very nick of time: and I know all. And no
other than myself shall be his wife. And indeed,

beyond a doubt I was the very wife he looks for, since everything corresponds, and exactly as he said; love has suddenly burst out flaming in my heart, at the very first sight of him, suddenly recollecting its old forgotten state. But whether I was his wife or not, in any other birth, I will very certainly become his wife in this. And all the symptoms conspire in my favour. For not only is my right eye throbbing, but I actually stumbled in ignorance on his very name, before I ever heard it. And now, I will, as Gangádhara said, set to work immediately without losing any time: for I know, as they do not, exactly what his wife is like. And now, everything will turn out well, so long as he never discovers in his life that I overheard him, on this terrace, before he ever saw me. And that cannot be, for he never can learn it from anyone but me.

So as she spoke, Arunodaya suddenly recollected the coming of the bird, and looked round, and rejoiced, to find that it was still there. And he said aloud, as if expressly to chime in with her thoughts: Ha! so, then, thou art not gone, as I feared. O sea-bird, from what far-off land art thou arrived? For none of the birds that haunt my palace resemble thee in the least degree. Art thou also looking for thy mate, as I am? Or hast thou lost thy way, blown by the winds over the home of monsters and of gems?

And instantly the bird replied: O King Arunodaya, not so: for I am looking neither for a mate nor a way: but have come here expressly, sent by the god, to tell thee how to find thy own mate, and thy own way.

And then, as Arunodaya started to his feet, scarcely crediting his own ears, she went on with that human voice: Listen, and do not interrupt, for I have overstayed my time, obliged to wait till thy conversation ended and thy minister was gone, and I have far to go. And tell me, first. Is there a little ruined temple, near thy city on the north, standing alone upon the shore? And Arunodaya said: There is. Then said Makarandiká: Then it all corresponds, and tallies exactly with my instructions. For only last night, as the sun was going down, I passed by a lonely island in the middle of the sea. And there in the evening twilight, I saw the Lord of Obstacles dancing all alone, throwing up his trunk that was smeared with vermilion into the purple sky. And he called to me as I was going by, and said: Carry for me a message to King Arunodaya, for thou wilt see his palace in the morning, standing up out of the sea, ruddy as my trunk in the early dawn. And tell him that I am pleased with his resolute perseverance: and by my favour he shall find the wife of his former birth. Let him go at midnight, on the fifteenth day of the light half of this very moon, into the ruined temple that stands on the shore of the sea, and I will put something in it that will fill his heart with joy.

And then, she rose from the terrace, and flew away across the sea: while Arunodaya stood still, gazing after her in wonder, till she dwindled to a speck and disappeared.

And then, he drew a long breath, and murmured to himself: Am I asleep or dreaming? Or can it really be, that the very Lord of Obstacles has been listening to my prayers, as well he might, considering their number, and taking pity on his devotee, has revealed to me the secret, by the means of this white bird: wishing to show Gangádhara, as if in jest, how easily the Deity laughs at obstacles that seem absolutely insurmountable, even to such a minister as mine?

IX

So then he waited, with a soul that almost leaped from his body with impatience, for the wax of the moon, which seemed to stand still, as if on purpose to destroy him. And he sent, in the meanwhile, a message to Gangádhara, saying: Everything is easy to those favoured by the Deity. And I have found what I was seeking, even without thy assistance, as I will prove to thee, by ocular demonstration, on the day of the full moon.

And as he listened, Gangádhara was so utterly confounded, that he could hardly understand. And finally, he said to himself: Beyond a doubt, this kingdom will presently be ruined, for the King is out of his mind. And now I begin to perceive, that it will become my duty to remove him from the throne, in favour of his maternal uncle, who is waiting and watching to devour him like a crab,[1] if only he can find his opportunity. Or is it only, after all, a device, to marry some girl that he has set his heart on, without consulting either policy or me? If so, let him beware! for he shall do penance for despising me, in full. But let me wait, in any case, for the moon to grow round. Yet what can the Lord of Herbs [2] have

---

[1] The crabs of Ceylon (presumably the same as those of southern India, whose shores I do not know) are the most extraordinary things I ever saw. They run like the wind, and jump, over immense spaces and chasms, from rock to rock, better than any horse.

[2] *i.e.* the moon.

to do with this matter, unless he possesses a medicine suited to the King's disease?

So then, at last, when the moon had gathered up all his digits but the last, as soon as he rose, Arunodaya went out of his palace to wander on the shore, with no companion but his sword. For he said to himself: What if it were all but a dream or a delusion? Then, were it to be known, I should become a very target for the ridicule of all the people in the city. So it is better to keep the secret to myself. And he roamed about the sand of the shore, near the temple, for hours, ready to curse both sun and moon together, the one for his delay in going down, and the other for taking such a time to climb into the sky. And finally, unable to wait any longer, he went directly, long ere midnight, to the temple, and stood for a while, exactly where yonder sleeper lies now, as if making up his mind. And at last, he came up between us, and peeped in, with a beating heart, and saw absolutely nothing inside, but emptiness and dark. And presently he said: Has that Lord of Obstacles deceived me, or is it too soon, for his present to arrive? And how will she come? Yet if that sea-bird was either a liar or a dream, it will be time enough to go away, before dawn returns, at any hour of the night. And he sat down at my feet, leaning his back against me, and looking out to sea, over which the moon was slowly climbing, exactly as it does to-night. And worn out with agitation, and fatigue, and suspense, he went off to sleep unawares. And he looked as he lay in the moonlight like the God of Love resting, after he had conquered the three worlds.

X

So then, when at last he woke, he lay for a little while puzzled, and trying to remember where he was, and why. And so as he lay, he heard suddenly behind him in the temple the faint clash of anklets, saying to him as it were : Thou art sleeping, but I am waiting. And like a flash of lightning, his memory returned ; and he started to his feet, and turned, and looked in at the temple door.

And lo ! when he did so, there, in a ray of moonlight that fell in through the ruined wall, and clung to her affectionately, as though to say: Here hiding in this dark cave have I suddenly fallen on my sixteenth digit that was wanting to complete my orb : there stood a young woman, looking like the feminine incarnation of the realisation of his longing to find the wife of his former birth. And she was leaning against the wall, half in and half out of the shadow, with her head thrown back against it, so that her left breast stood out in the light of the moon as if to mock it, leaving the other dark : and the curve of her hip issued from the shadow and again was lost in it, like that of a wave that rises from the sea. And he saw her eyes shining, as they gazed at him in curiosity, like stars in a moonless night reflected in a pool, whose light serves only to make the darkness it is lost in more visible than before. And her attitude gave her the appearance of a statue fixed upon the wall, that had suddenly emerged from it, and taken life, half doubtful, by reason of timidity, whether she should not re-enter it again. And she was dressed, like Jánaki, when the Ten-headed Demon seized her, in a robe of yellow silk, with golden bangles, and golden anklets, and a necklace of great pearls around her neck, like a row of little moons formed out of drops of the lunar ooze : and in her hair, which shone like the back of a great black bee, was a single champak blossom, that resembled an earthly star shedding fragrance as well as light. And her red lips looked as if the smile that was on the very point of opening like a flower had been checked in the very act, by the hesitation springing from a very little fear.

And Arunodaya gazed at her in silence, exactly as

she did at him. And after a while, he murmured
aloud, as if speaking to himself: Can this be in very
truth the wife of my former birth, or only a thing seen
in a dream?

And when he spoke, she started, and moved a very
little from the wall, with one hand resting still against
it, as if it was her refuge. And she said, in a low
voice: I thought the dreamer was myself. Art thou
some deity come to tempt me, and where am I, if it
is reality and not a dream? And Arunodaya said:
It is not I that am the deity, but thou. For who
ever saw anything like thee in the world? And yet
if thou art Shri, where is Wishnu? or if Rati, where
is Love?

And she looked at him steadily, and after a little
while, she said with a sigh: Alas! thou hast spoken
truly: where is Love?[1] What! can it be? and dost
thou not remember me? And Arunodaya said:
How could I remember what I never saw before in
my life? Then she said: What does this life matter?
Hast thou then so utterly forgotten everything of the
life before?

And as he gazed at her in perplexity, all at once
she started from the wall and ran towards him,
clapping her hands, and laughing, with her bangles

[1] *Love*, in Sanskrit, means also *recollection*.

and anklets and her girdle·clashing, as if keeping time with her movements, and exclaiming: The forfeit! the forfeit! I have won! I have won! And he said, smiling as if against his will: What forfeit? What dost thou mean? And for answer, she threw herself into his arms, and began to kiss him, laughing in delight, and crying out : I said it, I said it. I have remembered, and thou hast forgotten. Did I not tell thee, thus it would be, when we met again in another birth? Come, cudgel thy dull memory, and listen while I help thee; and after, I will exact from thee the forfeit that we fixed. And Arunodaya said again : What forfeit? For I remember absolutely nothing of it all. And she said: Out on thee! O thou of no memory at all. What ! is thy little pandit all forgotten? What! hast thou forgotten, what as I think could never be forgotten, how all the pandits shouted together at our marriage? And he exclaimed : Ha! pandits! Then she said : Ah ! Dost thou actually begin to recollect? then I have hopes of thee. But as to the forfeit, wilt thou actually persist in obstinately forgetting all about it? Must I actually tell thee, and art thou not utterly ashamed? Art thou not ashamed, after all thy protestations, to look me in the face?

And as she gazed, with eyes filled to the brim with

D

passionate affection that was not feigned, straight into his own, holding him with soft arms that resembled creepers, and as it were caressing him with the touch of her bosom and the perfume of the honey of her lips and her hair, taking him as it were prisoner by the sudden assault of irresistible flattery in the form of her own surrender, Arunodaya's head began to spin, lost as he was in a whirlpool of bewilderment springing half from her beauty's intoxicating spell, and half from ineffectual striving to recall at her bidding what she said, so that in his perplexity he could not even comprehend whether he recollected anything or not. And he murmured to himself: Surely she must be the wife I was looking for, for who else can she be? and certainly she is beautiful enough to be anybody's wife. And as he hesitated, balanced in the swing of indecision, she began to draw her forefinger over his eyebrows, each in turn, saying in a wisper: *Aryaputra,*[1] this was the forfeit. Give me thy hand, and shut, for a while, thy eyes. And as he did so, saying to himself: Now I wonder what she will give me: all at once he uttered a cry of pain. For she had taken his little finger with her teeth, and bitten it hard. And as his eyes flew open, as it were of their own accord, she

[1] A name given only by a wife to her husband, implying the claim.

said, with a frown and a smile mixed together: Why didst thou forget me? Was it not agreed between us that the forgotten should exact from the forgetter whatever penalty he chose?

And at the reproach in her eyes, the heart of Arunodaya began as it were to smite him, saying: Surely thou art but churlish in returning her affection, and refusing to remember her: for she is well worthy to be remembered. And being totally unacquainted with woman, and her sweetness, and her snare, his youth and his sex began as it were to side with her against his reason and his doubt, saying to his soul: What more canst thou possibly require in a wife, than such an incarnation of charm and affection and intoxicating caress. And all at once, he took her and drew her towards him with one arm about her slender waist, that a hand might have grasped, and the other round her head, and he began to kiss her as fast as he could, with kisses that she returned him till her breath failed. And after a while, he said, in a low voice: Who art thou in this birth, if as thou sayest, I was thy husband in the last? And hast thou fallen from the sky? For thou art altogether too different from the others, to be but a woman.[1] And what is thy name?

[1] The English reader may be puzzled by the difficulty: how

Then said Makarandiká: Thou art not absolutely wrong: for I am not a woman of the earth, but a Widyádharí, by name Makarandiká. And by and bye I will tell thee all about myself, and my coming here, to rediscover and regain thee; and learn of thee thine. But in the meanwhile, come outside this gloomy temple into the moonlight, where I can see thee. And she drew him out of the temple, and as they stood, looking at one another, she said: Dost thou know, that I am paying a great price for thee? See, a little while ago, I came hither flying through the air. And as I came, I said to myself, with regret: I am flying for the very last time: for to-morrow I shall forfeit all my magic sciences, by marrying a mortal. And as my resolution wavered, at that very moment, I arrived, and saw thee, lying asleep in the moonlight, at the feet of Maheshwara yonder on the wall. And instantly, I exclaimed: Away with these miserable sciences, for what are they worth in comparison with him, or, worse, without him?

And Arunodaya exclaimed: What! wilt thou sacrifice all thy condition as a Widyádharí for such

a Widyádharí could ever be a woman. But it is very simple on Hindoo principles. Widyádharas are constantly falling into human bodies by reason of curses, or guilt contracted.

a one as me? Out, out, upon such a price, for such a worthless ware!

And for answer, she took his hand, and put it on her heart, looking at him with eyes that shone not only with moonlight, but with a tear. And Arunodaya said, with emphasis: Thou must be my wife: for how could I think, having seen thee, of any other woman in the world, even in a dream.

And as he spoke, he started, almost uttering a cry. For suddenly she clenched the hand she held with a grip that almost hurt it, and he felt the heart it lay on suddenly leap, as it were, and stop. And as he looked at her in wonder, he saw her turning paler and paler, till she seemed in that white moonlight about to become a stone image, in imitation of ours, just behind her, on the wall.

And he said in alarm: Art thou ill, or suffering, or what? Or dost thou regret thy sciences? And then, all at once, she laughed, and said: My sciences? Nay, nay, it is not that, of which I am afraid. Come, it is nothing, and what am I but a fool? Let us go now to thy palace: and see, I will exert my power, for the very last time, in thy favour, and carry thee through the air. And she sat down on the step, saying: Come, thou art rather a large and a clumsy baby: yet sit thou on my lap. And she took him in her arms, and rose with him into the air, and they floated over the sea towards the palace, resembling for the moment myself and thee roaming in the sky.

And as they went, Arunodaya said within himself: Surely I am only dreaming; and of what is this Widyádharí made, that has claimed me for her own? Is it fire or something else?

But Makarandiká, as they floated, said to herself in ecstasy and exultation: Now, then, I have got him, and it will be my own fault, if I cannot so utterly bewitch him, as to cause him to forget all about his former wife, and take me, as why should I not have been? for her. And what do I care for her? For she may be the wife of that birth, but I am the wife of this. And why should the wife of the present count for less than the wife of the past?

III

A DISJUNCTIVE CON-JUNCTION

III

A DISJUNCTIVE CONJUNCTION

I

Now, in the meanwhile, it happened, that when all the other Widyádhara would-be bridegrooms had broken up and gone away in wrath, disgusted at being turned to shame by Makarandiká's rejection, there was one who went away with a heart that was more than half broken, for Makarandiká was dearer to him than his own soul. And he would have given the three worlds to have had the precious garland put round his own neck. And when all was over, he took himself off, and remained a long while buried in dejection on the slopes of the Snowy Mountain, pining like a *chakrawáka* at night-time for his mate, and striving to forget her,—all in vain : for his name was Smaradása,[1] and his nature like his name. And at last, unable to endure the fiery torture of separa-

[1] i.e. *the slave of love, or recollection.*

tion any longer, he said to himself: I will return, on the pretext of paying a visit to her father; and there, it may be, I shall at least get a sight of her. And who knows but that she may change her mind? for women after all are not like rocks, but skies. And at the thought, hope suddenly arose, reborn in his heart. For disconsolate lovers are like dry chips or straws, easily taking fire, and tossed here and there by the gusts of hope and desperation.

So as he thought, he did. But when he arrived at Mahídhara's home, and inquired about her, he received an answer that struck him like a thunderbolt. For Mahídhara said: As for Makarandiká, she has utterly disappeared, having gone somewhere or other, nobody knows where. And if, as I conjecture, she is looking for a husband among mortals, who will never even dream of any other woman than herself, she will not soon return. For it will be long before she finds him.

And then, that unhappy Smaradása said to himself: I will find her, no matter how long it may take me, if at least she is able to be found. So after meditating for a while, he went away to seek assistance from the brother of the Dawn. And he said to him: O Garuda,[1] I am come to thee for refuge. And it is

---

[1] The King of Birds. (The final *a* is mute.)

but a little thing that I ask, and very easy, for the Lord of all the birds of the air. There is a Widyádharí named Makarandiká, who is dearer to me than life itself. Help me, if thou wilt, to discover where she is: for she has disappeared, without leaving any trace.

Thereupon Garuda said: Stay with me for a little in the meanwhile, till I see what I can do. And he summoned all the sea-birds and the vultures in the world; and said to them: Go to the eight quarters of heaven, and find out what has become of Makarandiká, a Widyádharí who is lost.

So then, after a few days, they returned. And their spokesman, who was a very old vulture named Dirghadarshi,[1] said: Lord, this has been a very simple thing. For some of my people saw her, a little while ago, flying westwards. And following her track, on thy order, they saw her sitting on the palace roof of King Arunodaya, who has married her, and made her his queen.

And instantly, hearing this news, which pierced his ear like a poisoned needle, Smaradása uttered a loud cry, and fell down in a swoon: so great was the shock, that turned in the twinkling of an eye all the love in his soul to jealousy and hate. And when, with

---

[1] i.e. *long-sighted.*

difficulty, he came to himself, he hurried away so fast
that he forgot even to worship Garuda. But that
kindly deity only laughed, and forgave him, saying:
Well might he forget not me only, but everything in
the three worlds, on learning that his love was lying
in somebody else's arms.

But Smaradása summoned instantly all his brother
suitors. And he told them all about it, and he said:
This matter is no longer what it was. For if she
flouted us all, by refusing to choose a husband from
among us, yet no one could compel her, since she
did but exercise the privilege of all kings' daughters.
But now, not only has she placed this mortal above
us all, but by marrying beneath her caste, she has
degraded all the Widyádharas at once, and broken
the constitution of the universe. Therefore she
deserves to be punished. Moreover, she is at our
mercy, since she has lost all her magic sciences, by
marrying a man.

So then, when they had all unanimously pronounced her worthy of death, one suggesting one
death, and another another, Smaradása said scorn-
fully: What is the use of putting her to death? For
death is absolutely no punishment at all, since she
will abandon one body only to enter another.
Rather let us find some punishment suited to her

crime, and worse than any death. And the best way would be, to contrive some means of making her behaviour recoil upon her own head. And this could be done, if only we could get this husband she has chosen to desert her for another. For as a rule, a rival is like *kálakuta* poison to every woman: and she is not only jealous, but as it were jealousy itself. And thus she would become her own punishment. But first let us discover all about her: for then we can determine how to go to work.

So, when they all consented, Smaradása went back to Garuda, and he said: O Enemy of Snakes, do me one more favour, and I will trouble thee no more. Find out for me only, how matters stand with her husband and herself: since her independent conduct is a matter of concern to all the Widyádharas, of whom she is one.

And Garuda said: Smaradása, this commission is very different from the first. For if I am not mistaken, the Widyádharas mean mischief, and it is no business of mine. And yet, I will not do thee kindness by halves: but let this be the last. So after meditating for a while, he sent for the crows. And he said to them: Crows, you know everything about everybody, and see the world, and fly about the streets of cities, and eat the daily offerings,[1] and listen to all the scandal of the bazaars, and penetrate even into the palaces of kings. Go, then, to the city of Arunodaya, and spy about and listen, and bring back a full account of all you can discover, about him and his wife.

And, after a week, the crows returned. And their spokesman, who was called Kálapaksha,[2] said : Lord, this King and Queen are never apart, being as inseparable as Ardhanári.[3] And as for Makarandiká, it is clear that she is a *patidewatá*, who loves her husband more than her own soul. And though he has nothing to do with any woman but herself, yet something is wrong, though we cannot discover what it is. But the citizens think that she is jealous, because she suspects that he is always dreaming, not of her, but the wife of his former birth.

And as Smaradása listened, he exclaimed in delight : Ha ! what difficulty is there in doing a thing which is half done already? For this is a situation which will ripen almost without assistance, resembling

---

[1] *Balibúk, an eater of daily offerings*, is a common epithet of the crow.

[2] Meaning either *black-wings, the dark half of the lunar month*, or *time-server.*

[3] The combined form of Maheshwara and his " other half."

as it does a balance already trembling, in which the addition of a single hair will turn the scale. And it wants only a touch, for Makarandiká to turn her suspicions into certainties of her own accord. And thus she will become the instrument of her own torture, and expiate her error, the victim of her own choice, with nobody but herself to blame. For she was a Widyádharí, and is absolutely inexcusable.

II

And meanwhile Makarandiká, ignorant and careless of all that was occurring in that world of the Widyádharas which she had thrown away like a blade of grass, and utterly forgotten, was living like a siddhá in a moon without a spot, having, so to say, attained emancipation in the form of the husband of her own choice. And for his part, Arunodaya, having lit upon the very wife of his former birth, contrary to expectation, and married her again, lived with her like one plunged for an instant in an ocean of intoxication, salt as her beauty [1] and infinite as her devotion, and unfathomable as her eyes. And for a while, he seemed to be the very image of a bee drowned in the honey of a red lotus, or a *chakora* surfeited with

[1] A play on words, *salt* and *beauty* being the same (*lawanya*).

the beams of a young moon. And in order to make up to Makarandiká, and console her for the loss of her power of flying through the air, which of all her sciences she most regretted, he built for her innumerable swings, with gold and silver chains, and one, that she loved the best, on the very roof she first arrived on. And she used to pass her time in it, whenever she had nothing else to do, swinging softly to and fro, and looking across the sea; tasting, by means of the swing and her own imagination, some vestige of her lost equality with all the birds of heaven. And though she never so much as whispered it aloud, yet sometimes, her unutterable longing to possess once more that power which she had lost for ever, as she watched the sea-birds flying, brought tears into her eyes, which she never let Arunodaya see.

And yet, though she had utterly lost all her magic sciences, she still retained the whole of that other magic, which the Creator has not limited only to Widyádharís, of feminine fascination. And like the moon, she was a very bundle of bewitching arts,[1] whose potency was doubled by the intensity of her affection for her lord. For a woman who does not feel affection for her own husband resembles a sunset from which the sun and all his redness are withdrawn.

---

[1] *Kalá* means *arts* as well as *digits*.

And she was, moreover, so absolutely bent upon erasing from his recollection every vestige of the dim image of the wife of his former birth, for whom she had substituted herself, like a new moon eclipsing an old one, that she thought of nothing else: and the thought of this former wife resembled a thorn that was fixed ineradicably in her own heart. And she busied herself all day and night, in occupying his whole attention, and laying snares for his soul, by dancing, and singing, and telling him innumerable stories, and making as it were slaves of all his senses, enthralling his eyes with the variety of her beauty, and captivating his ears with the sorcery of her voice, and chaining his desires to herself by never-ending wiles of caressing attention, in the form of embraces of soft arms, and kisses like snowflakes, and glances shot at him out the very corner of her eye, enveloping him with such a mist of the essence of a woman's sweetness as to keep him from seeing any other thing at all. For her Widyádharí nature gave to all her behaviour grace that was far beyond the reach of any ordinary mortal, and she seemed like an incarnation of femininity, divested of all the grossness and clumsy imperfection that it carries when mixed with the element of death, so that her touch seemed softer, and her step seemed lighter, and her outline rounder,

E

and her smile far sweeter and her passion purer, and her whole love ecstasy deeper and truer than any woman's could ever be.

But as for the prime minister, when he came, according to agreement, and Arunodaya showed her to him on the day of the full moon, he was so utterly bewildered by the very sight of her that she turned him as it were to stone. And after staring at her in stupefaction, being wholly bereft of appropriate speech, and as it were deserted by his reason, which lay prostrate at her little golden-bangled feet, he went away in silence. And after a long while, he said to himself as he sat alone : Beyond a doubt, this inexplicable King has somehow or other managed to find a very miracle of a queen, as far as beauty goes. For her very ankles alone, are enough to drive a lover mad, and worth more than the whole body of any other woman ; so that whoever began to look at her, beginning with her feet, would never get any higher, but remain for ever worshipping their slender and provoking curve, with a thirst that was never quenched. She must be Rati or Priti, fallen, nobody knows how, into a mortal birth, and leaving Kama in despair. And yet, whether she be, as he supposes, the very wife of his former birth, or not, I am irretrievably disgraced. For he has managed this matter all alone, without so much as consulting me. And thus, not only have I lost my opportunity, of taking as it were tribute from all the surrounding kings, but I am very much mistaken if some of them, or even all, will not take umbrage at the slight put upon all their daughters by this unrelated queen,[1] and band together, and suddenly attack him, bewildered as he is by her disastrous intoxication; and so, the kingdom will be uprooted, since he is likely to be so entirely wrapped up in her that he will think of nothing else. And it may be that he will discover in the future that he has lost more, by disregarding his prime minister, than he has gained, by marrying even for the second time the wife of his former birth. And if, as I suspect, this is all but a trick, time will show up the imposture, and then it will be my turn. For if ever he should discover she has cheated him, all the coquetry and coaxing in the world will not keep him from abhorring her, for stealing his affection, and diverting it away from its proper object, to herself. For as a rule, men object to being cheated, even to their own advantage, since the cheater seems to argue that the cheated is a fool. But in the meantime I must wait, since it is useless to do anything, till the charm has lost its magic by dint of repetition. For beauty resembles amber:

---

[1] Every reader of Scott will recall the "kinless loons."

it attracts, but does not hold : and like a razor, loses virtue every time that it is used : till at last, it becomes altogether blunt, and impotent, and without either edge or bite. And then, unless I am very much mistaken, this lovely false wife of his previous existence will find, that she has to reckon with a formidable rival, in his recollection of the true.

III

But Arunodaya, careless of his minister, gave himself up a willing captive to the witchery of his Widyádharí wife. And for a time, her task was very easy. For owing to his inexperience, he resembled a child, and every woman was to him an illusion, and a mystery, so that he would have sunk under the spell, even had it been less potent than it actually was. And Makarandiká was as it were his *dikshá*,[1] incarnate in a form of more than mortal fascination : and like a priestess she took him by the hand and led him into the *garbha*[2] of that strange temple built not of stone, but of the materials of elementary infatuation, and made him perform, so to say, a *pradakshina* round

[1] *i.e.* initiation.
[2] The Greek ἄδυτον, or sanctuary.

the image of the divinity [1] of which she was herself a
bewildering and irresistible incarnation.   And lost in
the adoration of a neophyte, he lay like a drunken
bee in a lotus-cup, rolling in honey, and forgetting
utterly not only his kingdom and its affairs, but everything else in the three worlds.

And yet, strange! there lay all the while lurking in
the recesses of his soul a vague misgiving, mixed
with a faint and unintelligible dissatisfaction, resembling a taste of something bitter in the draught of his
infatuation, and an ingredient that qualified and just
prevented his gratification from reaching its extreme
degree, of ecstasy without alloy.   And yet he hardly
dared to acknowledge it, even to himself, accusing
himself of ingratitude and treachery, and saying to his
own soul: How is it possible to requite such infinite
affection, and devotion, and service, and beauty, by
returning nothing in exchange for it all but suspicion,
and distrust, and doubt?   For even if she were not
the very wife of my former birth, what could I possibly
wish for, more?   And yet, it is very strange.   For notwithstanding all she does, she does not seem to reach
and satisfy the craving for recognition in my heart,

[1] The Hindoo shrine, says Mr. A. K. Coomaraswamy, is
essentially a place of pilgrimages and circumambulations, to
which men come for *darshan*, to "see" the god.

which obstinately refuses to corroborate her assevera-
tions : nor do I ever feel that confidence and certainty,
arising from the depths of recollection, which, if she
really were my former wife, surely I ought to feel. Is
it my fault, or hers? Alas! instead of meeting her
half-way, I am oppressed with what is very nearly dis-
appointment, and feel almost like a dupe, that have
allowed myself to fall into the snare of beauty, so as
to yield to another what should belong to one alone.
Little indeed would she have to complain of in the
warmth of my return, had she just that one thing that
she lacks, the stamp of genuine priority : for then
she would get in full the very thing I long to give her.
Aye! I am as it were dying to do, the thing I cannot
do, and divided from supreme bliss by a partition
composed of the most exasperating inability to know
for certain, what all the time may after all be true.
For if she is only playing a part not really hers, how
in the world did she discover the way to take me in,
by exhibiting a knowledge of those very same dim
vestiges of recollection which I have never told to
anyone but my own prime minister? And very sure
I am, that it was not he who told her, since he almost
lost his reason with astonishment, and admiration
that was mixed with envy and annoyance, when her
beauty struck him dumb. So after all, perhaps I am

mistaken, and only torturing myself for nothing. Out
on me, if what she says be really true! for then indeed
I deserve something even worse than death, for treat-
ing her with such monstrous ungenerosity. Can it be
that her memory is truer and stronger, putting mine, for
its fidelity, to utter shame? Or why, again, should I
struggle any longer against conviction, and persevere
in longing for what I have not got? Who knows
whether even if I actually got it, I should be any
better off than I actually am? Could the very wife of
my former birth be a better wife than this? Is not
this wife just as good as any wife could ever be? Does
she not as it were combine the virtues of even a
hundred wives? Yet if she be not the true, can it be
that the other is even now upbraiding me, somehow,
somewhere, for falling with such inconstancy straight
into another's snares, and wasting on a stranger the
love that belongs to her? Alas! alas! Why did the
Creator make my memory too strong for blank oblivion,
and yet so feeble as to leave me without a proof, and
plunge me in such perplexity in this matter of a wife?

IV

So then, time passed, and these two lovers lived
together, she in the heaven of having discovered the

very fruit of her birth, and he half in heaven and half outside, hovering for ever between delight and discontent, balanced in a swing of hesitation between assertion and denial, that like that other swing of hers was hardly ever still. And little by little, as surfeit brought satiety, and custom wore away the bloom of novelty, and familiarity began to rob her beauty of the edge of its appeal, and emotion lost, by repetition, its sincerity, and passion's fire began to cool, and the flood of desire to ebb, then exactly as that cunning Gangádhara foretold, the doubt that, like a seed, lay waiting in his soul began, seeing its opportunity, to swell and grow, till there came to be no room for any feeling but itself. And unawares, he used to sit gazing at her, with eyes that did not seem to see her, as if continually striving to compare her with some other thing that was not there, till under their scrutiny she shrank away and left them, unable to endure, turning away a face that became paler and ever paler, half with apprehension of discovery, and half with jealousy and resentful indignation : for only too well her heart understood what was passing in his soul, though he never dared to tell her, out of shame at having to confess, that in return for the free and absolute gift of her soul, he was yielding her only a fragment of his own, and even that, with suspicion and reluctance : converting the very completeness of her surrender into an argument against her, as if she did from policy alone what came from the very bottom of her heart. And he seemed to her to say by his behaviour : Did she not throw herself into my arms uninvited, without even waiting to be asked, of her own accord, like an *abhisáriká*, and could such a one as this be really the wife that I was looking for? Does it become a maiden, even a Widyádharí, to be bolder than a man? And why is it, that for all that she can say, and all that she can do, she never can succeed in arousing any corresponding sympathy, or producing a conviction that we ever met before? And is this the union I expected, devoid of that overwhelming mutual recognition that would leap like fire out of the darkness of oblivion, if the associations of a previous existence were really there?

So she would sit thinking, and watching him furtively, sitting in her swing, and swaying gently to and fro, gazing out over the sea. And she used to say sadly to herself : Now, as it seems, all my endeavours have been fruitless ; for do what I can, all my labours are unavailing. And I have given myself away, and sacrificed all my magic sciences, for nought. For it is clear that he cares for absolutely nothing, in comparison with this dream of this wife of his previous birth. And yet what could she, or any other wife whatever, give to him, or for him, more than I have given. What! is the wife of the present birth so absolutely less than nothing, compared with the wife of the past? What! has not one birth the same value as another? And if she was the wife of that birth, then I am the wife of this. Very sure I am, that she cannot love him as well as I. Have I not become, from a Widyádharí, a mortal, solely on his account. And yet, who knows? For it may be, I am impatient, and am hoping to succeed, too soon; anticipating, and expecting to pluck the flower of his full affection before the seed that I have sown has had full time to grow. Well then, I will water it, and watch it, and let it ripen. And I will strive, in the very teeth of his prepossession, to overcome his stubborn recollection, and uproot it, not by ill-humour or peevish premature despair, but by flooding him with all the sweetness that I can. Yes, I will conquer him by becoming so utterly his slave, that for very shame he will find himself obliged to sacrifice his dream to me.

V

So then, as she said, she did. And making herself as it were of no account, and utterly disregarding the absence of reciprocal affection in a soul that held itself as it were, with obstinacy, aloof, she set herself to thaw his ice by a constancy of service that resembled the rays of a burning sun. And she met all his suspicion and his scrutiny by such invariable tenderness, and with such a total absence of even the shadow of complaining or reproach, that his heart began, as if against its will, to melt, unable to hold out against the steady stream of affectionate devotion, welling from an inexhaustible spring. And little by little, he began to say to himself as he watched her: Surely it were a crime to doubt her any longer. For such an irresistible combination of unselfishness and beauty could not possibly flow from any other source than the unconscious reminiscence of old sympathies, and adamantine bonds, forged and welded in a previous existence. For she gives and has given all, in return for almost nothing, resembling a mother rather than a wife; and so far from resenting any lack of confidence, she makes up for all that I do not give her, by increasing the quantity and quality of her own, as if she had incurred an obligation to myself, in some former and forgotten state, which she was never able to repay. And what proof other than this could I demand? And if this good fortune of mine, in her form, be not the reward of works, done in that birth which I struggle to remember, what else can it be?

So then at last, there came a day, when they sat together in the twilight on the palace roof, watching the moon, that wanted only a single digit, rising like a huge nocturnal yellow sun, looking for the other that had sunk to flee, far away on the eastern quarter, on the very edge of the sea, which seemed for fear to tremble like an incarnation of dark emotion, while a lunar ray, like a long pale narrow finger, ran over straight towards them, stepping from wave to wave, and seeming to say with silent laughter: Like me on the surge of the deep's desire, love bridges over the waves of time. What is the tide without me, but the livery of death?

And as she gazed, the eyes of Makarandiká shone, for very excess of happiness, and there came into each a crystal tear, that caught and reflected the moon's ray, like a twin imitation of himself. And as she looked, she murmured: Now at last, as I think, the victory is all but mine, for I have never brought my husband yet so near the very edge of love's unfathomable deep, as I have to-day. And now, with just one more effort, he will fall into the bottomless abysses of my soul, and I shall have him for my own. Strange! that she did not understand, she was herself tottering on the very brink of a fatal gulf that would swallow her up for ever, and plunge her, by a single step, into the mouth of hell!

For even as she spoke, she turned, and looked for a single instant, with unutterable affection, into her husband's face. And then, she said aloud: *Arya-putra,* dost thou know, of what I am now thinking? And he said: No. Then she said: How short a time it seems, since I settled on that parapet in the form of a sea-bird, and saw thee first: and yet, the difference is eternity!

VI

And then, the very instant she had spoken, re-collection suddenly rushed across her: and she knew, like a flash of lightning, that she had uttered her own doom. And as she gazed at him with eyes, whose love suddenly turned to terror, Arunodaya, all at once, started to his feet. And he exclaimed: Ha! wert thou the bird? Ha! now, at last, I understand. So this, then, was the means of thy discovery, and the origin of thy deceit, thy listening to the conversation of my minister and me? And all thy story was a lie, and thou thyself art nothing but a liar and a cheat. And like a worm, that is hidden in the recesses of a flower, thou hast placed thyself on a

king's head, being only fit to be cast away and
trodden underfoot: as I myself will tread thee, and
cast thee away like a blade of grass, fit only to be
burned. And I will sweep the very shadow of thy
memory from my heart, into which thou hast wriggled,
by treachery and fraud, to the prejudice of its proper
owner, the true wife of my former birth.

So as he spoke, with eyes that consumed her, as
it were, with the fire of their hatred and contempt,
she stood for a single instant still, stupefied and
aghast, shrinking from his fury, and confessing by
her confusion her inability to clear herself of the
charge he brought against her, looking like a feminine
incarnation of the acknowledgment of guilt. But
as he ended, the thought of the rival whom he
cast into her teeth entered her heart like the stab
of a poisoned sword. And as he looked at her,
all at once he saw her change. And the fierce fire
of his own emotion suddenly died away, annihilated
as it were and turned in a trice to ashes as he
watched her, by the intensity of hers. For from
crouching as she was, she slowly stood erect, becoming so ashy pale that life seemed on the very point of
leaving her a thing composed of snow and ice in the
white rays of the moon. And she looked at him with
eyes, in which the love of but a moment since had

frozen into a glitter, as though the blood that filled her heart had suddenly turned to venom that was black instead of red. And so she stood for a moment, and then all at once she leaped at him and clutched him by the hand, with fingers that shut upon it and squeezed into it like teeth. And she said, with difficulty, as if the breath were wanting to make audible the words : Dost thou repay me thus? And have I thrown away my state of a Widyádharí, and all my magic sciences, for such a thing as thee, and this? And have I sacrificed a countless host of suitors, who would have given the three worlds for a single glance of my eye, for thee to trample on my beauty and my affection, counting it all as absolutely less than nothing, in comparison with another who is nothing but a dream? Make, then, the very most of all the sweetness and the love that she will give thee; for mine thou hast lost, and it is dead, and it is gone. See, whether the affection of the wives of thy future and thy past will make up to thee for that of thy wife of the present, which thou hast despised, and outraged, and mangled and annihilated, and wilt never see again.

And she turned, abruptly, and looked for a single instant away across the sea. And she said :

I cannot leave thee as I would have done, for I have lost my power of flying through the air. But bid adieu to the wife of the present, and sing hey! for the wife of the past.

And as she spoke, her voice shook. And she went away very quickly into the palace, and left him there on the roof alone.

VII

Now in the meanwhile, the prime minister was well-nigh at his wits' end. For ever since his marriage, Arunodaya had entirely neglected his kingdom and his state affairs, throwing upon Gangádhara the burden of them all. And this would have been exactly to his taste, in any other circumstances but those in which it happened : since it was just the very marriage itself which occasioned all his anxiety and care.

And one day as he sat alone, musing in his garden, at last he could contain himself no longer, but broke out into exclamations, imagining himself alone. And he said : Ha ha! now, as I feared, this lunatic of a King and his mad marriage are about to bring destruction on this kingdom and myself. And as to my own part, it would be bad enough alone, that I should have lost not only crores of treasure, which I could easily have gained, but also the opportunity of making favourable political alliances with the strongest of the other kings. But even worse things are impending over the kingdom and myself. For not one only, but all the kings together are collecting to attack us, considering themselves slighted; and as I am made aware, by means of my own spies, the King's maternal uncle is in league with them in secret, hoping by the ruin of his nephew to secure the kingdom for himself. And between them, I also shall be crushed, since they consider me as one with the King my master; and it will all end in my losing, not only my property, but my office and my life : since I cannot even get this King to listen, were it only with one ear, to any business at all : and without him, there is nothing to be done. Thus I myself, and he, and his kingdom, will all go together to destruction, like sacrifices offered to his idol, in the form of his wife. And yet there is something unintelligible even in his relations with his wife, which even my spies are unable to detect. For though the King and Queen are never separate, even for a moment, yet they do not seem to be at one : and though he has got, as it seems, exactly what he wanted, yet he does not appear to be content. Something, beyond a doubt, is wrong, though nobody can discover what it is. And in the meantime, we shall all presently discover something

F

else, that we are all involved in a common catastrophe : and very soon, it will be too late, even to hope to take any measures whatever against it at all. For as a rule, delay is fatal at any time : but above all now. And I cannot see any other way than to throw in my lot with the King's maternal uncle, and so save the kingdom and myself, at the King's expense. And if I do, he will have absolutely nobody to blame but himself, for having scouted me and my policy, and like a mad elephant rather than a king, imagined that he was at liberty to marry anyone he chose, behaving just as if he were a subject, and not a king with political necessity to consider, before any private inclination. And now, could I only discover some means of bringing it about, I should be more than half resolved to oust this unmanageable King from his throne. But the difficulty is, how to get rid of him and his strange windfall of a queen, without incurring suspicion and the blame of the bazaar. For I can get no satisfactory solution of this mystery, even from my spies.

So as he spoke, all at once a voice fell out the air upon his head, as if from the sky. And it said : O Gangádhara, there are ready to assist thee other and far better spies than thy own.

VIII

And as Gangádhara started, and looked up in wonder, he saw Smaradása just above him, hovering in the air. And that celestial roamer descended gently, and stood upon the ground beside him. And he said to the prime minister, who humbly bowed before him: Gangádhara, I am Smaradása, a king of the Widyádharas, and I have come to let thee know so much as may be necessary, and tell thee in this matter what to do: which is, to sit with thy hands folded, like an image of Jinendra on a temple wall, for a very little while, and the conclusion will arrive of itself, without thy interference: since others are concerned as well as thou, in punishing this king, and his outcast of a queen, who like a wheel has left the track, and run out of her proper course, downhill.

And Gangádhara said: My lord, I am favoured by the very sight of thee: and I am curious to know all the circumstances of this extraordinary matter, if it be permitted to such a one as me.

And Smaradása said: O Gangádhara, creatures of every kind fall into disaster by reason of their own characters and actions, and this is such a case. And there is no necessity for thee to be acquainted with any of the particulars, since curiosity is dangerous, and those who pry into the business of their superiors run the risk of getting into trouble, which they might have avoided had they been discreet. So much only will I tell thee, that this queen's independent behaviour is on the eve of giving birth to its own punishment, which will in all probability involve in it that of her silly lover as well as her own. And the Widyádharas have fixed upon thee, to be an agent in bringing it about. And I bring thee a commission, which if thou dost refuse, evil will come upon thee, very soon, and very sudden, and very terrible. But as I think, thou wilt undertake it, seeing that the result will tally precisely with objects of thy own. For as I said, spies better than thy own have had their eyes on thee and all the others, unobserved.

Then Gangádhara trembled, and he said: This servant of thine is ready to do anything, no matter what.

And Smaradása said: There is little to be done, and it will be very easy. Know, as it may be that thou knowest already, that Arunodaya desires nothing in the world so much, as to recollect the incidents of his previous existence: since this is what perpetually troubles him, that he seems to be hovering for ever on the very brink of grasping recollection, which nevertheless invariably slips from his grasp: leaving

him in such a state of irritated longing and disappoint-
ment, that to quench it, he would give the three
worlds. Go, then, to Arunodaya, and give him this
fruit. And say to him this: Maháráj, one of the
neighbouring king's ministers, whom I have recently
befriended, sent me this fruit, with its fellow, brought
to him by a traveller from another *dwipa.*[1] And such
is their virtue that whoever eats one, just before he
goes to sleep, will dream, all night long, of the very
thing that he most desires. And so, wishing to test
it, I ate one ; and that night I saw in my dreams such
mountains of gold and gems, that even Meru and the
ocean could not furnish half the sum of each. And
now I have brought thee the other, thinking that the
experience might amuse thee: and now it is for
Maháráj to judge. And when he hears, Arunodaya
will think the fruit to be no other than the very fruit
of his own birth in visible form before his eyes. For
it will enable him to realise his desire, and discover
the events of his former birth.

And Gangádhara took the fruit into his hand, and
looked at it attentively, resembling as it did a pome-
granate, but smaller. And the smell of it was so
strong, and so strange, and so delicious, that it
seemed to say to its possessor : Refrain, if you can,

---

[1] (Pronounce *dweep*)—a far-off continent or island.

from tasting, what tastes even better than it smells. And then, he shuddered, and he raised his eyes, and looked steadily at Smaradása: and he said: Is it poison?

And that crafty Widyádhara laughed, and he said: Nay, O Gangádhara: it is exactly what I told thee to say, and thy account will be the very truth.

Then said Gangádhara again: But if this is so, how can Arunodaya's eating it advantage either thee or me?

And Smaradása said: Gangádhara, it is dangerous for anybody, and much more for this King, to recollect his former birth, even in a dream. Beware of eating it thyself: for it is tempting. But now, mark very carefully what I have to say. See, when thou dost give it him, and tell him, that the Queen is by. I say, mark well, that at the time of thy telling, she overhears thee: and beware, at thy peril, of forgetting this condition, for in it will all the poison of the fruit be contained; and without it, it is naught.

Then said Gangádhara: I do not understand.

And Smaradása laughed, and he said: Gangádhara, no matter: for thy understanding is not an essential condition of success. But be under no concern: for Arunodaya will not die of poison, and the fruit is free of harm. For poison of the body is a very clumsy contrivance, and one suited only to mortals who are void of the sciences, not knowing how or being able, like Widyádharas, to work indirectly by poisoning the soul.

IX

So then, Gangádhara did very carefully just as he was told. And everything came about exactly as Smaradása had predicted. For the soul of Arunodaya almost leaped out of his body with delight, in anticipation of the satisfaction of his curiosity, by making trial of the fruit; while the lips of Makarandiká grew whiter, and shut closer, at the sight of it, as if it contained her rival in its core.

And that very night, Arunodaya went up upon his palace roof, according to his custom, to sleep. And he took with him the fruit, which he carried in his hand, not being willing to let it out of sight for a moment, for fear that Makarandiká might steal it, in order to thwart his expectation, and prevent him from having as it were an assignation with any other woman, even in a dream. And as it happened, that night a strong wind was blowing from the east, and the waves of the sea broke against the rocks of the palace foot, as if they were endeavouring to move it from its place.

And while Arunodaya threw himself upon his bed, Makarandiká went and sat, a little way away, in her swing, that rocked and swayed to and fro in the wind, looking out across the sea, with gloom in her eyes: and casting, every now and then, glances at him as he lay, out of the corner of her eye, that seemed as it were to say to him : Beware ! And like her body, her soul was tossed to and fro in the swing of un- utterable longing and despair. And she said to herself: Even in my presence, which he absolutely disregards, he is preparing for a meeting in his dreams with this wife of his former birth. And at the thought, she frowned, and turned paler, clutching tighter unawares the chains of her swing, and setting her teeth hard, and casting at Arunodaya, lying in his couch, as it were daggers, in the form of dark menace from eyes that were filled with misery and pain. And the moon in the first quarter of its wane seemed as it were to say to her : See, thy power is waning, exactly like my own.

And in the meanwhile, Arunodaya took his fruit and ate it, and lay down, with a soul so much on tiptoe with desire and agitation that sleep seemed to fly from him as if on purpose, out of sympathy with her. And for a long while he tossed to and fro upon his bed, listening to the roar of the waves and the wind. And so as he lay, little by little he grew quiet, and sleep stole back to him silently and took him unaware. And his soul flew suddenly into the world of dreams, leaving Makarandiká alone in the darkness, awake in her swing.

X

But Arunodaya fell into his dream, to find himself walking in a row of kings, into a vast and shadowy hall. And as they went, that hall re-echoed with a din that resembled thunder : and he looked, and lo ! that hall was as full of pandits as heaven is of stars, all dressed in white with their right arm bare, and each so exactly like the other that it seemed as though there was but one, reflected by the innumerable facets of a mirror split to atoms, all shouting together, each as loud as he could bawl: See, see, the suitor kings, coming to marry the pandit's daughter ! Victory to Sarojiní, and the lucky bridegroom of her own choice !

And as Arunodaya looked and listened, all at once there rushed upon his soul as it were a flood of recollection. And he exclaimed in ecstasy: Ha ! yes, thus it was, and I have fallen back, somehow or other, into the bliss of my former birth. And there once more, I see them, the pandits and the hall, exactly as they were before, all shouting for Sarojiní. Aye! that was the very name, which all this time I have been struggling to remember. And strange! I cannot understand, now that I recollect it, how I should ever have forgotten it, even for a single instant. But where then is she, this Sarojiní, herself?

So as he spoke in agitation, he looked round as if to search, and his heart began to beat with such violence that he stirred as he slept upon his couch. And at that moment, there suddenly appeared to him a woman, coming slowly straight toward him, followed by her maid. And as she came, she looked at him intently, with huge, bewildering, gazing eyes that seemed to fasten on his soul, filled as they were with an unfathomable abyss of melancholy, and longing, and dim distance, and dreamy recognition, and wonder, and caressing tenderness, and reproach. And her body was straight and slender, and it swayed a little as she walked, like the stalk of the very lotus whose name she bore, as if it were about to bend, unable to support the weight of the beautiful fullblown double flower standing proudly up above it in the form of her round and splendid breast. And she was clothed in a dusky garment exactly matching the colour of her hair, which clung to her and wrapped her as if black with indignation that it could not succeed in hiding, but only rather served to display and fix all eyes upon the body that it strove to hide, adding as if against its will curve to its curves and undulation to all its undulations, and bestowing upon them all an extra touch of fascination and irresistible appeal, by giving them the appearance of prisoners refusing to be imprisoned and endeavouring to escape. And as it wound about her, the narrow band of gold that edged it ran round her in and out, exactly like a snake, that ended by folding in a ring around her feet. And she held in her right hand, the arm of which was absolutely bare, an enormous purple flower, in which, every now and then, she buried, so to say, her face, all except the eyes, which she never took from Arunodaya, even for a single instant. And she seemed to him, as he watched her, like a feminine incarnation of the nectar of reunion, after years of separation, raised into a magic spell by an atmosphere of memory and mystery and dream.

So as he gazed, lost in a vague ocean of intoxication, all at once her attendant maid, who seemed for her boldness and her beauty like a man dressed in woman's clothes, or some third nature that hovered between the two, came out before her mistress. And she seized by the hand a suitor king, and led him up to Sarojiní, and said to him aloud : O King, listen and reply to the question that the husband of Sarojiní must answer well.

And as she spoke, Sarojiní withdrew her eyes from Arunodaya, and let them rest for a moment on the king that stood before her. And she said in a low voice, that sounded in the sudden stillness of that hall like the note of a *kokila* lost in the very heart of a wood : Maháráj, say : should I choose the better, or the worse ? [1]

And that unhappy king said instantly : The better.

Then said Sarojiní : O King, I am unfortunate indeed, in losing thee.

And instantly, she turned her eyes back upon Arunodaya, and at that moment, all the pandits in the hall began to shout : Sarojiní, Sarojiní, *jayanti!* And as he listened, lo ! she and her eyes, and the hall with all its pandits, wavered, and flickered, and danced before his eyes, and went out and disappeared. And the clamour and the tumult of the pandits changed, and altered, and melted into the roar of the waves and the wind. And in a frenzy of

---

[1] This cannot be expressed in English with the point of the original, because the word expressing preference means also *bridegroom* (*waram*).

terror lest the dream should have concluded, he woke
with a cry, and raised his head from its pillow,
and opened his eyes; and they fell straight upon
Makarandiká, who was looking at him fixedly, sitting
in her swing. And suddenly she said to him: Of what art thou
dreaming? And he answered: Of pandits. And
immediately, his head fell back upon its pillow, and
his soul sank back into his dream.

XI

But Makarandiká started, and she exclaimed within
herself: Pandits! Ha! Then, as it seems, he really
is dreaming of the things of his former birth. And
her eyes grew darker as she watched him, sitting in
her swing, very still, with one foot upon the ground.
And all at once, she left the swing, and came to him
very quickly, and knelt, sitting upon her feet, upon
the ground, beside him, gazing at him in silence as he
slept, with eyes that never left his face for even a
single instant.

But the soul of Arunodaya, leaving his body lying
on the couch, flew back like a flash of lightning eagerly
to his dream. And once more he found himself in
that hall, with all its pandits shouting, just as if he

had never left it to awake. And lo! the eyes of Sarojiní were fastened on his own, as if with joy; and in his relief, occasioned by sudden freedom from the fear of the dream having reached its termination, and the recovery of those eyes, his heart was filled with such a flood of ecstasy that, all unaware, he laughed in his sleep. And in the meantime, that unabashed and clever maid came forward, and seized by the hand another king, and led him forward like the last. And she said, exactly as before: King, listen and reply to the question that the husband of Sarojiní must answer well.

And then once more, the eyes of Sarojiní lingered for a little on those of Arunodaya, and left him, as if reluctant to depart, and rested, as if carelessly, upon that second king. And she said in the silence that waited, as it were, for her to speak: Maháráj, say, shall I choose the greater or the less?

And that unhappy king hesitated for an instant; and he said: The less.

Then said Sarojiní: Alas! O King, once more I am unfortunate: for I should be inexcusable, in choosing thee.

And instantly, she turned, and her eyes met those of Arunodaya, waiting in the extremity of agitation, with a glance that seemed to say to him : Be not afraid.

And as he sighed in his sleep, for delight, lo! once again, she and her eyes, and the pandits, and the shouting, and the hall, shivered, and wavered, and receded into the darkness, and went out and disappeared. And the din of the triumph of the pandits changed and altered and ended in the roar of the waves and the rushing of the wind. And once more he awoke and opened his eyes: and lo! there just in front of him was Makarandiká, with eyes that gazed, as if with wrath, straight into his own.

And when she saw his open, she said in a low voice, very slowly: Of what wert thou dreaming? And Arunodaya murmured: Of pandits. And instantly, he closed his eyes, as if to shut her from his soul. And then, he forgot her in an instant, and flew back, as if escaping from a pursuer, into his dream.

XII

But Makarandiká's face fell. And after a while, he began to laugh, with laughter that quivered, as if it hesitated between agony and scorn. And she exclaimed: Pandits! Does anybody laugh, as he did in his sleep, who dreams of pandits? What has laughter such as his to do with pandits? Nay, he is trying to hide from me a secret, not knowing, that in the absence of his soul, his body is playing traitor to him against his will. Ah! well I understand, he closed his eyes, to keep me on the outside of his soul, which he opens in the sweetness of a dream to someone else. So, now, let him beware. And she drew still closer to his side, and leaned over him, with her eyes fixed upon his lips, and a heart that beat with such agitation that she pressed one hand upon her breast, as if to bid it to be still, lest its throbbing should rouse him from his sleep.

And as she gazed, there came over her soul such a sense of desolation, mixed with the fire of jealousy, and wrath at her own inability to follow him into his dream and snatch him for her own from everybody else, that her breath was within a little of stopping of its own accord. And she yearned to find, as it were, a refuge, in tears that refused to flow, and her head began to spin. And all at once, a shudder that was half a sob shook her as she kneeled, mixed with an almost irresistible desire to clasp him in her arms, and claim him for what he actually was, her husband, and the only lord without a rival of her own miserable heart. And a fever that turned her hot and cold by turns began to hurry through her limbs. And she murmured to herself, without knowing what she said : Shall he leave me here, deserted, alone in the darkness of this palace and the night? to meet in a dream where I cannot follow him the wife I cannot oust from his soul? Who knows? It may be that at this very moment, they are laughing me to scorn, locked in each other's arms.

And so as she continued, gazing at him with a soul set as it were on fire by suspicion and images of her own creating, and a heart stung by the viper of recollection, and yet, strange! swelling with a passionate and hopeless yearning for his affection to return, meanwhile, the soul of Arunodaya, all heedless of the passion that menaced his abandoned body, lay, as it were, drowned in the honey of his dream. And once again, amid the tumult of the pandits, the eyes of Sarojiní were drawing his soul towards her own, as if with cords, woven of the triple strands of colour and reminiscence and the intensity of a love that was returned tenfold. And so as he lay, conscious of absolutely nothing but the abyss of those unfathomable eyes, all at once that shameless maid came forward yet again, and took the hand of yet another king, and said as before : King, listen and reply to the question that the husband of Sarojiní must answer well.

And Sarojiní, hearing her speak, drew her eyes away sadly from Arunodaya, and turned them slowly on

G

that waiting king. And she said: Maháráj, say, shall I choose the bitter or the sweet?

And then, that miserable king, as if he feared the fate of his predecessors, stood for a while in silence. And he said at last: The sweet.

Then said Sarojiní: King, beyond all doubt my crimes in a former birth are bearing fruit, in depriving me of such a husband as thyself.

And instantly, all the pandits broke into a shout, and as they did so, she shot at Arunodaya a glance that seemed as it were to say to him: Be patient, for thy turn also will presently arrive.

And at that very moment, something took him as it were by the throat. And as the dream suddenly went out and disappeared, he awoke, in the roar of the waves and the wind, to find that Makarandiká had her hand upon his breast, to wake him from his dream. And she said absolutely nothing. But her eyes were fixed upon his own, filled to the very brim with entreaty, and affection, and terror and grief, and despair.

And seeing her, he frowned, as if the very sight of her was poison to his soul. And he shut his eyes, and fell back upon his pillow, to go back to his dream.

XIII

But Makarandiká shrank from the glance that he cast upon her, exactly as if he had struck her in the face with his clenched hand. And she turned suddenly white, as if the marble floor she sat on had claimed her for its own. And all at once she fell forward, and remained, crouching, with her face upon her hands, like a feminine incarnation of Rati when she saw Love's body burned to ash. And time passed, while the moon looked down at her as if with pity, wondering at her stillness, and saying as it were in silence : Can it be that she is dead? And then, suddenly, Arunodaya laughed aloud in his sleep, and he murmured, as if with affection : Sarojiní, Sarojiní.

And then, Makarandiká looked up quickly. And lo! there came over her a smile, like that of one suddenly rejoicing at the arrival of unexpected opportunity. And all at once she stood erect, as if all her agony had been changed in a moment to resolution. And she looked down at him as he slept, and she said, very slowly : Ah! lover of Sarojiní, dost thou leave me, as it were, spurned from thee with aversion, alone on the roof of thy palace, to spend thy time with her? What! shall the wife of this birth sit, weeping as it were outside the door, while she embraces thee within? Ah! but thou hast forgotten, that if I cannot enter, at least I can interrupt thee, since I am mistress of the dream.

And she put her hands up to her head, and undid the knot of her braided hair. And she took from it, as it fell around her, as if to shroud her action in the darkness of a cloud, a long thin dagger,[1] that resembled a crystal splinter of lightning picked up on a mountain peak, and shone in the moon's rays like a streak of the essence of vengeance made visible to the eye. And she went close up to him, and remained standing silent, watching his face turned upwards as he lay before her, with a smile on her lips that resembled the gleam of her own dagger, as it waited in her trembling hand.

XIV

But in the meanwhile Arunodaya fled as it were from Makarandiká to take refuge in his dream. And he found Sarojiní as it were waiting for him with anxiety, with eyes that seemed to say to him: Amidst all this tumult of the pandits, thou and I are as it were

"Did not Windumatí slay Widuratha the Wrishni with a stiletto that she had hidden in her hair?" (*Harsha charita*).

alone together. And it seemed to Arunodaya as he
watched her, that her lips moved, and were striving
to say to him something, that by reason of the distance
and the shouting, he could not understand. And in
his delight, he began to laugh in his sleep, and
murmur back to her in answer : Sarojiní, Sarojiní.
And filled with unutterable desire to approach her,
and take her in his arms, he was on the very point
of rushing forward, urged by the irritation of an
impatience that was becoming unendurable, when
once again that maid devoid of modesty came straight
towards him, and almost broke his heart in two by
taking by the hand not himself, but the king who
stood beside him. And as he muttered to himself:
Out on this interloping king, who comes between me
and my delight! beginning to tremble all over as he
lay, that maid said again : King, listen and reply to
the question that the husband of Sarojiní must
answer well.

And Sarojiní turned half towards him, leaving as it
were her eyes behind, fastened still on Arunodaya, as
if unable to bear again the pain of separation, and
calling as it were to him, from over the sea of time.
And then she said, as if her words were meant for
him alone! Maháráj, Maháráj, say, shall I choose
the past or the present, the living or the dead?

And then, ere that unhappy king could answer, Arunodaya leaped towards her, while all his body quivered as he lay upon his bed, as if struggling in desperation to accompany his soul. And he cried out, not only with his soul, but his body: Sarojiní, Sarojiní, never shall thou choose, since I will not leave the choice to thee at all. Dead or living, I am thine and thou art mine. And as she threw herself into his arms, he caught her, and pulled her to his breast, while she put up her face to him, as if dying to be kissed.

And then, strange! that face suddenly eluded him, with a derisive sneer. And his ears rang with a din composed of the shouting and laughter of pandits, mingled with the roar of the wind and the sea. And she and the dream together suddenly went out and disappeared. And he saw her face, for the fraction of a second, change, as if by magic, into the face of Makarandiká, pale as ashes: and then, something suddenly ran into his heart like a sword. And his soul abandoned his body, with a sharp cry, never to return.

XV

So then, the very moment it was done, Makarandiká woke, herself, as it were, from a dream. And horror at her own action, as if it had waited till the very moment when it should be unavailing, suddenly flowed in upon her soul. And as she gazed at Arunodaya, lying still in the moonlight with her dagger in his heart, and found herself with absolutely no companions but the dead body, and the darkness, and the wind and the waves, alone on that palace roof, she murmured to herself, as if she hardly understood : What! can this be of my doing? What! have I actually slain the husband of my own choice, jealous of his very dreams?

And she stood, for a little while, with one hand upon her head, and then, she uttered a scream. And she seized him by the hand, and shook it violently, as if endeavouring to wake him and recall him from a dream, in which she herself had buried him for ever, cutting off its termination, and prisoning his soul in an everlasting dungeon, like a stone dropped beyond recovery, fallen with a hollow echo into the black darkness of a well.

And lo! that shriek reverberated as it were in heaven, and was answered by a peal of laughter that fell on her from the sky. And she looked up into the air, and saw, hovering in rows above her, all those Widyádhara suitors whom she had rejected long ago, gazing down at her with faces that were distorted with malice and derision. And as she stood, confounded, with their laughter ringing in her ears, Smaradása swooped towards her, and called to her ironically: Ha! Makarandiká the scornful, how is it with thy mortal husband? How could he prefer another to such a beauty as thyself?

And Makarandiká gazed at them all for an instant, with eyes that exactly resembled those of a fawn, on the very verge of escaping from its pursuers by leaping from a cliff. And her reason fled away from her, as if anticipating her own flight. And strange! at that moment, as if bewildered by her own deed and the very sight of those Widyádharas of whom she had been one, she utterly forgot for an instant that she herself was no longer a Widyádharí, and had lost her own power of flying through the air. And she made a bound to the edge of the parapet, and leaped off, thinking to fly over the sea, and escape, and be at rest. But instead of flying, she fell, and was broken to pieces at the bottom of the wall, in the foam of the waves that were also broken, at the foot of the palace rock.

––––––––

So then, when at last Maheshwara ended, the Daughter of the Mountain asked eagerly: But, O thou of the Moony Tire, tell me, how as to the dream. Was it the very truth, and Sarojiní the very wife of his former birth?

And Maheshwara said slowly: Nay, O Snowy One, not at all. For it was not even a true dream. For if it had really been a dream, it would not have continued, as it actually did, in spite of its interruptions. But the whole was a delusion, and a contrivance of the Widyádharas, who lured his soul out of his body by means of a magic drug, and acted all before him, exactly like a play. For the Widyádharas were the pandits, and the great hall was nothing whatever but the sky. And the noise was nothing whatever but that of the wind and waves, and Sarojiní herself was Makarandiká's own sister, who hated her for her beauty, which was greater than her own. And as for Makarandiká, she was all the time her own rival; for she herself, and no other, was the real wife of his former birth.

And the Daughter of the Mountain started, and she uttered a little cry. And she exclaimed: Ah! no! O Moony-crested, it cannot be. Surely thou art only jesting? What! was their happiness divided from them by so thin a wall as that? What! when they would have given, each his soul, to know it? Alas! alas! what cruelty of the Creator, to bring the cup of happiness as it were to their very lips, without allowing them to taste! simply by reason of a film of utter darkness, that prevented them from seeing it was actually there!

And after a while, that Lord of Creatures said slowly: O Daughter of the Mountain, yet for all that it was true. And many a traveller crosses over seas and years of separation, surmounting every peril, to perish at the very last moment, when the ecstasy of reunion is almost in his grasp, on the step of his own door. And be not thou hasty to lay cruelty to the door of the Creator, who is absolutely blameless in the matter, seeing that all these and similar misfortunes come about, as the necessary consequence of works. And though the extremity of happiness, arising from mutual recognition, was divided from Arunodaya and Makarandiká by a screen thinner than the thickness of a single hair, they could not reach it, for thin as it was, that screen had been erected by their own wrong-doing, and was nothing whatever but the doom pronounced against themselves by their own misbehaviour in a former birth. And thus it came about, that Makarandiká played the part of Arunodaya's former wife, never even dreaming that she was only claiming to be what she actually was: while Arunodaya shrank, in his ignorance, from the very wife whom he would have given the three worlds

to discover, in pursuit of a phantom, that was substituted for her by his own unilluminated longing for
a treasure that, all unaware, he held already in his
hand. For souls that wander to and fro in the waste
of the world's illusion resemble chips tossing aimlessly
up and down on the heaving waves of time, driving
about at random they know not how or where, under
a night that has no moon, in an ocean without a
shore : for whom the very quarters of heaven are lost
in an undistinguishable identity, and even distance
and proximity are but words without a sense.

So, now, let us leave these our images to become
once more, by our departure, nothing but the stony
guardians of this empty shrine. And to-morrow
Gangádhara will learn, by listening to the story of
yonder sleeper, what Smaradása meant, and unriddle
his enigma of the poisoning of the soul.

Lightning Source UK Ltd.
Milton Keynes UK
UKOW02f2326090816

280348UK00001B/46/P